ROAD TO REDEMPTION
A Bunker® World Series

Published by BookBreeze.com LLC
November 9, 2020

ISBN: 9798561771262

Written by: Jo Nash & Jay J. Falconer

Foreword by USA Today
Bestselling Author ML Banner

Welcome to *Bunker: Road to Redemption*. This story is a creative collaboration between USA Today Bestselling Author Jay J. Falconer and veteran author Jo Nash, whose tireless pursuit of excellence and dedication to the incredible story of Jack Bunker shines through on these pages. They worked together for over a year on this story and we hope it exceeds all of your expectations.

This prequel takes place in the days just before the unstoppable Jack Bunker got on the train in Colorado. Not only will you learn how Bunker selected his name, you'll witness how the invasion plan took shape in Russia.

I hope you enjoy what you're about to read. It's one non-stop action sequence after another and I think you'll enjoy the ride, so to speak.

The authors' plan is to make this a three-book spin-off series, so don't forget to post a review and let them know what you think about this story.

Jo Nash, Jay J. Falconer, M.L. Banner

Your feedback will help them determine if they should continue this new series or not. So please, post a review and tell them what you think of this story.

Now it's time to strap yourself in and prepare for another amazing *BUNKER*® adventure.

—ML Banner

CHAPTER 1

Valentina Zakharova stepped in front of two well-muscled Russian guards and pointed down the hallway as they dragged Marc Reynolds through the door, smacking his head on the wall.

"Hey! What the hell? I'm on your side, remember?" Marc said in English.

Valentina watched the American software developer-turned-Russian spy twist his head, looking at her with his good eye. The other was swollen shut, his lower lip glimmering with a fresh hue of red.

Marc licked the blood from his lip. "Right, good-lookin'? Tell them, tell them I'm on your side."

That's when the guards stopped cold, and one of them spun around, landing a punishing punch to Marc's gut.

Marc sucked in a few short, painful breaths as he slid lower in their grasp.

Valentina detested anyone who mentioned her looks. She knew what everyone thought—that she landed her job as General Zhukov's Russian interpreter and personal assistant because she was blonde and drop-dead gorgeous. But she knew the truth—she was damn good at her job.

She leaned down and twisted Marc's ear, yanking his head toward her. "I would save your words for the General," she said in perfect English, her tone sharp. "And by the way, whatever it is you have to say—it better be good."

Valentina gave his ear one last tug, allowing the guards to continue ushering him to the General's office.

The squeaking of Marc's sneakers on the polished floor made Valentina's jaw clench. It reminded her of her grandfather. He was a strict, distant man with beady eyes, a retired college professor who loved to use his fingernails on a chalkboard—or on any surface within his reach as he aged—to get everyone's attention.

She forced a grin when they reached the General's door, then knocked twice.

A guttural grunt came from behind the door. Valentina understood the General's grumble. She had to—her job depended upon being able to interpret that man's every word, gesture, and even his primal sounds. And when the General was consumed with a mission, caveman-speak was the prevalent form of communication.

She turned the knob and stepped inside, holding the door open for the guards. They dragged Marc into the room and stood at attention, waiting for instructions.

The General's office was the epitome of stark—a plain maple desk with a single pen next to a white coffee mug, a non-swivel office chair with years of wear on its cloth upholstery, and a detailed, unframed world map that hung at an angle on the wall.

Valentina walked over and stood behind General Zhukov. It was customary to do so during meetings such as these. She preferred formality.

The General looked up from his paperwork and nodded to a single chair in front of his desk.

Once the guards deposited Marc into the chair, the General waved them out. Valentina closed the door behind them.

Marc had gotten his breath back and he started right in, with his immature and disrespectful American ranting—at the General, no less.

"Dude, you really need to bring your guards up to speed. Look, I'm on your side. And yet they still did this. Seriously?" he asked, pointing to his eye with a trembling hand. "And get this, simply because I called Valentina good-looking—*bam!* they punched me. What's that all about?"

The General took two strides to Marc and smashed his fist into Marc's nose. Blood dripped in spurts, engulfing the lower half of Marc's face.

"No talk about Officer Zakharova!" the General said in broken English, pointing his index finger in Marc's face.

Marc held up his hands in surrender, as blood continued to ooze from his nose. "Okay, okay. I got it." He wiped his face on the sleeve of his shirt, wincing from the pain.

Valentina watched as the look of concern on Marc's face turned to terror. Maybe the American traitor was realizing that his status on Team Russia was not as concrete as he had thought.

The General nodded to Valentina, indicating it was time for her to take over the interrogation.

She marched forward with a crisp step. "General Zhukov would like to know if you have located Angus Cowie or Misty Tuttle?"

Marc's eyes went wide, then he looked at Valentina, then at the General, glancing at each of them several times in silence.

"Answer!" the General said, his accent thick.

"Uh, you said not to talk to her."

Valentina held back a smirk as the General sighed, his eyes glaring at Marc with impatience.

"Govorit'!" the General said through clenched teeth.

Valentina knew Marc didn't speak much Russian, even though he'd been in the country long enough to have picked up some of the local dialect.

Marc surprised her when he answered—she still wasn't sure if Marc understood what the General said or if the General's tone was enough to make anyone talk, in any language. "Like I kept telling those mutant guards of yours—who do not listen, by the way. You know, I think they just like to torture people. I could've told them I had U.S. nuclear launch codes and they still wouldn't have listened. And I still don't understand why I was treated like the enemy. I'm. On. Your. Side."

The General puffed out his chest, then clasped his hands behind his back.

Marc continued. "Look, at first I thought I had a solid lead about Cowie and Tuttle, but it turned out to be a dud. I have another source I can check out, but I ran out of time. I didn't want to be late for our meeting."

"So you *do* have information for the General? Who is this new lead?" Valentina asked.

Marc shrugged. "I didn't get a chance to meet with her yet, but I will. I swear. I will."

"When? The General is tired of all these delays."

"Soon. I just need a little more time."

General Zhukov looked at Valentina.

She shook her head.

The General held up a firm hand, his fingers pressed together in a tight formation, then fixed his stare at the ceiling.

Valentina moved to the side; she knew what was coming next.

It only took a millisecond for the General to pull his gun out of the holster and aim it at Marc's head.

"No! Wait, please!" Marc said, his eyes filling with fear.

The General pulled the trigger. The sound of gunfire tore through Valentina's ears. Marc's body knocked the chair over as it flew back against the wall. His torso stood atop his legs for a moment, then wobbled before sliding down, leaving a trail of blood on the paint as the corpse fell to the floor.

Valentina remained quiet, looking from the bloody mess to the General, his expression unwavering. Marc should have gotten the job done. He had been given plenty of opportunities. For some reason, the American always preferred to test the General, tempting fate one too many times.

Before her next breath, a knock rang out from the door.

The General nodded, giving her the go-ahead.

She stepped over the fallen chair, walked to the door, and opened it.

A young man, wearing a crisp uniform, stood at perfect attention with his eyes locked on the top of the door frame. He held out a manila envelope with General Zhukov's name written on it.

Valentina took the envelope in one hand, then put the other out, latching her fingers around the knob, ready to close the door.

"Wait," the General said in Russian.

Valentina let go of the knob and turned away from the door.

"You. Clean this up," he said to the budding soldier, waving his hand at Marc's remains as if it were roadkill stinking up his office.

The boy hesitated, waiting to see if the General would say anything further, she guessed. When the General didn't, the kid looked at Valentina.

She answered, also in Russian. "Bring a mop and bucket, as well as a large roll of plastic from supply. Make it quick, soldier. And bring someone back to help carry the body."

The boy was halfway down the hall before she closed the door and shifted her focus to the General. He had the envelope open and the papers inside were now spread across his desk.

She watched a grin spread across his face from ear to ear.

He slapped his hand on the wood and let out a bark of laughter, then pointed to the top of the page.

Valentina leaned in and read the words written on the order:

Operation Clean Sweep Approved.

Immediate Deployment.

Full Battalion.

Clearwater, Colorado. United States of America.

CHAPTER 2

Tess Wainwright yanked the front door of the American Center in Moscow open and headed into the lobby.

"Hi Tess," Rosa said, tossing her apple core in the garbage and pulling at her impossibly tight skirt. Impossibly tight skirts and high-heeled shoes were the extent of Rosa's uniform, donned everyday—even in the dead of the Russian winter. Tess secretly would have loved to have long, beautiful legs like Rosa's, but it seemed a little too risqué for a center focused on the educational welfare of the local community. "Heard you turned down the Director's job."

Tess nodded, but didn't respond.

"Too bad, you would've been good at it," Rosa said, winking.

Tess smirked, then took an envelope out of her satchel and put it on the desk. "Would you turn these forms in for me, please?"

"Sure thing. Oh, and Senator Spaulding left a message. He wants you to call him. Said he's been trying to reach you. Sounded kind of urgent. He's a bit of a jerk, if you ask me," she said, handing Tess a message slip.

Tess took the pink paper from her. "Yeah sorry, my uncle can get like that. He seems to be under a lot of stress. I wonder why he didn't call my cell?"

"If your phone's acting anything like mine the last couple of days, that could be why. Signal sucks. Maybe try outside."

She tucked the note in the side pocket of her satchel, then hiked it up on her shoulder. "Thanks for the message." Rosa smiled in response, her teeth bright white against her raspberry-colored lips.

Tess left the building as quickly as she came in, then took out her phone. No signal. Not a single bar. Usually, as soon as she stepped out of the Center she would be prompted to pick a wireless network. It used to drive her crazy but at that moment, she would've welcomed the pop-up.

She walked the length of the square outside, testing the signal in a number of places, even trying a block down the street. Nothing changed. The cell towers must have been down. Time for Plan B.

Tess went back inside, where she found the check-in desk surrounded by volunteers looking at their phones. They were having trouble as well, she guessed.

"Any luck?" Rosa asked.

"Not even one bar," Tess said, shoving her phone into her bag.

"Well, that stinks. Hey, I forgot to mention to you earlier Misty called yesterday after you left. Said she would be out sick today."

"Misty who?"

"She's your new class assistant," Rosa said, handing her Misty's volunteer paperwork.

"Oh, that's right, sorry. Misty Tuttle. She volunteered to help with my fencing class."

"What's up with volunteers lately? I mean, really—sick on her first day?" Rosa asked, in a tone filled with sarcasm.

"She could actually be sick, you know."

"I say she's just a flake."

Tess raised an eyebrow. "You don't even know her."

"Whatever."

The front door opened and Rosa pointed to the delivery guy walking toward them. "Watch out. Here comes hottie-hot delivery guy."

He set a large box on the floor next to the desk. It was impossible to tell what was in it, and the shipping label was written in Russian. "Sign, please," he said in choppy English.

"Sure thing, hon," Rosa said, winking.

Tess rolled her eyes. "Thank you," she said to him in Russian.

Rosa watched him walk back out the front door before grabbing the scissors to open the box. "Let's see what we have here."

"Maybe it's my new fencing masks."

"Ta-da." Rosa held up one of the masks. "Five of them. I'll log them in for you."

"Thanks. Only five? I was hoping for nine."

"Budget cuts. The Director sent out that memo, remember?"

"These are the times I really miss being able to hop on Amazon and place an order."

"Hey Tess, is your cell working?" one of the volunteers asked, as she continued to stare at her iPhone.

"Nope. I'm heading upstairs to try the landline. Man, I hope it works."

"What the—? Now the computer isn't working," Rosa said, slapping the desk in frustration and knocking the mouse to the floor. It smashed into pieces and the battery rolled under the desk. Rosa glared at the pieces scattered at her feet before picking up the desk phone and putting the receiver to her ear. "Switchboard is down, too. What is going on?"

Rosa hung up the phone, then bent down and scooped up the pieces of the mouse, putting them on the desk. She tapped Tess on the arm, nodding at the entrance. "Speaking of hottie-hot."

Tess turned around to see her most loyal student—Dominik. He was headed straight toward her, with just a hint of a smile.

"The kid needs to learn how to smile."

Tess frowned at Rosa. "Leave him alone."

"Oh brother. Just admit that you like him, Tess."

"He's way too young for me."

17

"Right, a whole two years younger. Really?"

"Really. And besides, I'm his teacher."

Rosa shook her head, tucking a strand of her shoulder-length ebony hair behind her ear. "Whatever you say. But I'd be his cougar anytime."

Tess put up a hand, blocking her view of Rosa's face. "Please stop, you're grossing me out."

"I'm just saying have some fun. Life is way too short."

Tess pulled her hand down and smiled when Dominik stopped in front of the desk. "Hi Dom."

"Hello Tess," Dom said, in a thick Russian accent. He turned to Rosa. "Miss Rosa."

Rosa smirked.

He pointed to the shipping box sitting on the floor. "Are those the new masks?"

"Sure are. Just arrived," Tess said, pulling her phone back out of the satchel to see if by some miracle it was working, but by the somber expressions on the volunteers' faces, she knew there wasn't much hope.

Dom stared at Tess while she checked her phone. "Is something wrong?" he asked, leaning closer to her.

"The phones and computers aren't working," Tess said, trying to play it off as nothing, even though her gut was screaming it was definitely something. "You'll have to wait to sign in until after we figure out the computer problem, okay?"

"All right, sure. No problem."

Tess—feeling the need to get in touch with her uncle—turned to Rosa. "I'm going to take the masks upstairs. Let me know when the computers are back up, would ya?"

Rosa nodded once. "Will do."

"If you don't want to carry them all the way up there," Dom said, "you can use the dumbwaiter. I don't mind helping."

Tess bent down and picked up the box. It was heavier than she expected. She grunted without meaning to, having to lean her back into it. "Thanks, but I can manage."

"I'll go with you, just in case," Dom said, holding his arms out to take the box.

Tess hesitated, looking at Rosa and then at the girls, all of them giggling at the interaction. She wasn't in the mood to argue, so she let Dom take the box before they headed toward the stairs at the end of the lobby.

"So how are things at the lab? Did you get your project done?" Tess asked the tall, blonde, blued-eyed Russian, making it to the top of the stairs before he did.

"Project?" he asked, hesitating on the step below.

"Last week you mentioned you were behind on some project for the lab and had to work late."

"Right. Right. Sorry. Everything is fine," he said, looking down and holding his gaze on his feet.

Before Tess could respond, she heard a high-pitched screech, then several muffled slamming sounds, followed by a series of loud pops. It came from outside, but from where exactly, she couldn't tell. Might have been a car accident—someone in a hurry slammed on their brakes and hit a truck, she figured.

Just then, the door to the dance studio flew open and the instructor ran out, tailed by her students—the young girls screaming as they pushed their way toward the stairs.

"What's wrong?" Tess asked, stepping in front of the teacher.

"They're shooting at everyone!" the elderly woman said, her eyes filled with tears.

"Who is shooting everyone?" Tess asked.

The woman didn't answer, slipping her arm around the little redheaded girl who was wrapped around her leg and guiding her toward the stairs.

Tess didn't hesitate, running into the studio and heading straight for the nearest window.

Dom joined her a few seconds later, dropping the box on the floor and looking over her shoulder at the street below.

A convoy of Russian trucks and troops had cordoned off the street in both directions. All Tess could see were bodies on the ground and people running as they poured out of the building and into the street. And guns. Lots of guns, in the hands of the soldiers.

The troops fired into the crowd, cutting down innocent people as they ran in every direction at once.

Tess jerked away from the window, stopping short when she felt Dom's chest against the back of her head. She couldn't believe what she'd just seen, her breath disappearing from her lungs in an instant. "Why are they doing this? Dom, how can they just kill them like that?"

"I don't know," Dom said, taking her hand. "Let's go. We need to get out of here."

When they reached the bottom of the stairs, Dom crouched, then pulled Tess close to him against the inside wall and peered over the handrail, just as three Russian guards stormed through the front door with rifles at the ready.

One of the guards aimed his gun at Rosa. She ducked down behind her chair, while inching her way to the other side of the check-in desk, her back to the door. He pulled the trigger without hesitation, shooting Rosa in the back. She flew into the wall, a splatter of red covering the paint-cracked surface.

Tess gasped—putting her hand over her mouth—then watched as bullet after bullet took the lives of friends and colleges as they ran for cover.

"Find the Americans. Find them now!" the lanky guard stationed near the door said in Russian, waving his weapon toward the ceiling.

"Americans? Why do they want Americans?" Tess asked Dom, moving a little closer to him. She understood Russian pretty well, but maybe she hadn't heard the guard correctly. "Please, tell me I heard him wrong. Tell me they're not searching for Americans?"

"I wish I could, but you heard it right. I just don't understand why they're shooting everyone."

Bile rose up in Tess' throat as Rosa's blood streamed out of her motionless body, making an oozing pool of red. She fought back the urge to vomit, knowing if she didn't keep it together and figure a way out of this building, this would be her last thought. "We need to get out of here, now!"

Dom pointed at the gunman in the lobby. "We can't go that way. We'll never make it."

"What about the break room? There's an emergency exit that leads to the alley."

Dom shook his head. "That's the first place they'll position troops, expecting people to make a run for it."

"Not if we hide first. Wait them out. They'll have to leave eventually, right?"

"Maybe, but where? They're going to search the building."

"I have an idea. You know the stage in the drama room?" Tess closed the space between them so

Dom could hear her better. "It has a crawl space underneath—the youth class would go under there and come up out of the trap door in the stage floor for surprise entrances during performances. It's the best place to hide."

Dom nodded, his eyes locked on Tess' mouth. "Okay, come on."

They crept along the back side of the staircase and slipped past the break room to the hallway on the other side of the pass-through, making it to the drama room without being discovered.

Tess could still hear the echoes of gunshots coming from the front part of the building, knowing that each pull of the trigger meant the slaughtering of more of her friends. The shooting never let up. Not for a moment, which meant more blood and guts sprawled across the lobby floor.

Her heart wanted her to stop and mourn the victims, but her mind wouldn't allow it. Survival had to come first.

Once inside the drama room, Tess ran past the costume boxes toward the main curtain. She pulled it aside, searching for the access panel.

The hallway filled with the sound of guards opening doors, then the soles of their boots clomping on the floor as they searched for American targets.

Tess hurried to the far end of the stage and slid to her knees. She removed the panel, then dragged her body underneath.

Dom did the same, then stuck his fingers through the grille and repositioned the panel before dragging his body farther back and wriggling next to her.

There were streaks of light leaking in through gaps in the panel, which made it easier for them to see and maneuver around. But it might also give them away.

Her heart started to race at the thought that maybe she'd made the wrong call. That her plan would position them as easy targets. Two more for the body count—well, at least one—her—since it was clear that they were only looking for Americans.

When Dom reached her, he twisted to match her position from behind, then wrapped his arms around her waist.

Tess sucked in a breath, not expecting him to make that move even though it did lessen their footprint under the corner of the stage.

Perhaps it was his way of making her feel safe and—despite everything she once said about Dom making her feel uncomfortable when he was close—it did.

The sound of boots entering the room tore her from her thoughts. Both of their bodies stiffened as they listened to the clatter of gear and equipment, and the grunts of soldiers searching the room.

That's when she remembered the trap door near the rear of the stage. Eventually they'd see it and look inside. If the guards shined their flashlights anywhere near them, they'd be discovered for sure.

Tess tapped Dom on the shoulder and pointed up. "Trap door," she mouthed, her eyes growing wide.

Dom looked around, then nodded toward the opposite corner of the stage, where a support pillar for the building stood. "Behind there. Go. I'll distract them," he said in a deep whisper, brushing his lips over her ear.

She twisted her neck to look at him. "No way," she whispered, shaking her head.

Dom pointed to the corner over and over again. His eyes flared when she didn't move. His hands flailed, demanding she hide—waving toward the sound of the soldiers' footsteps, then at the trap door, indicating that the Russians were going to find them hiding here.

Once again, she shook her head. He may not have been an American, but her gut told her those guards would kill him, too.

Dom rolled off the floor, hovering over Tess. She wrapped her fingers between the buttons on his shirt and drew him in, kissing him on the lips.

When she pulled away, Dom's eyes flared wide before unwrapping her fingers from his shirt and pressing them to her chest.

Tess knew there was no changing his mind.

He turned his head toward the pillar and gave her a nudge.

She crawled across the cold cement with tears in her eyes. She pulled her body in behind the pillar, tucking her legs underneath her.

Dom waited until Tess disappeared into the shadows of the pillar, then inched his way to the trap door.

When he unhooked the latch and flipped the door open, he was met by the barrel of an assault rifle. An AK-47, if he wasn't mistaken.

"Don't shoot!" Dom said in Russian. "I'm not American."

The guard pushed the barrel of his weapon against his head. "Get out of there. Let's go!"

Dom braced his hands on the floor of the stage and hauled himself out of the hole and onto his feet. He waited until the guard gave him the go-ahead before he bent down and lowered the hatch back in place.

"Step back, slowly," the guard said, flicking his rifle in the direction of Dom's feet.

Dom did as he was instructed.

"Let me see your papers."

Dom went to his pocket and slid his ID out at a slow pace, then showed it to the soldier.

"Citizen, what are you doing here?" the man asked, his square jaw making an odd clenching motion, as if he were chewing gum.

"I was here for a class and heard the gunshots, so I hid."

"Are you alone?" the guard asked, leaning over to look behind him.

Dom was about to answer, but the Russian didn't wait for it. The man stooped, opened the flap and peered under the stage floor. He took out a flashlight and turned it on, aiming the beam inside.

Dom held his breath while the soldier scanned the substructure of the platform, sweeping his light from one section to the next.

Fifteen seconds ticked by until the guard straightened up, turning off his light.

Dom let the air out of his lungs, keeping a close watch on the man's facial expression in case the guard had spotted Tess during the crawlspace search.

Dom needed the troops to focus on something else. Something not in this room. That's when he remembered Tess mentioning the storage room was being remodeled for its transformation into an information center.

"You might want to try the room just past the stairs. It's being renovated," he told the other guards, hoping they'd take the bait.

After conferring with the lead Russian, two of them departed and the last man ushered him out of the room.

Tess waited about thirty minutes before she slid out from under the stage. She hadn't heard voices, boots, or gunshots in a while, so she headed for the rope that opened and closed the main curtain.

The rope hung from a support rod above, its extra length coiled on the floor like a snake. She tugged on it, opening the curtain all the way, then put her weight into it and yanked hard.

The rod above buckled, sending the rope to the floor. She dragged it behind her to the dumbwaiter that Dom had suggested she use earlier instead of carting the box of fencing masks up the stairs.

She pulled the access door open with her hand. A loud metal-on-metal screeching sound clawed at her ears but she ignored it as she slapped the Up button.

She knew the mini-lift wouldn't start to move until the door was sealed tight, which gave her time to toss the rope inside and fold herself in and on top of the platform. Good thing she was small in stature, because there wasn't a lot of extra room.

The drama room door swung open and another soldier ran in. He caught sight of Tess before she could pull her legs all the way in.

She slammed the access door shut and slid to the back of the lift.

The man opened fire, tearing holes in everything above, below, and all around her as the dumbwaiter began to move upward.

Just then, a searing pain tore at her thigh. She wanted to cry out, but clamped her mouth shut as she looked down and saw blood leaking from her leg.

The guard yelled a string of demands before he started pounding on the door—probably with his fist or the butt of his rifle; she wasn't sure. Nor was she sure why the Russian hadn't realized that with a little force, he could've opened the access door.

Tess squeezed her hand around the wound as she willed the lift to go faster. It didn't take long before a strange groaning sound erupted above her, then the dumbwaiter rocked hard, tipping to one side. "No. Not now, just get me to the top," she whispered to herself.

The lift slowed a few seconds later, just as the sound of a cable breaking rang off the walls in a ping, causing the platform to swing backwards.

She figured the soldier hit the cable with one of his bullets. It must have only partially frayed, then completely unraveled under the strain, leaving the dumbwaiter wedged in the shaft sideways.

Tess knew if she waited, the lift might plummet, so she pushed herself up to her knees and peered up to see that the dumbwaiter had stopped several feet from the access door on the top floor.

She took the rope she'd snatched from the curtain rod and tied it around her waist, then got to her feet and lunged, grabbing onto the bottom ledge of the door frame. It took every bit of her strength, but she was able to pull herself up and force the door open.

The room she climbed into was an office assigned to the Director of the Center—a man who wasn't around much, but when he was, things got done.

Tess picked up one of the many picture frames sitting on his desk. It was of the Director standing in the middle of a white-capped river, his smile broad as he displayed an enormous salmon, holding it firmly from mouth to tail. "So that's where he's been going," she said under her breath, then put the picture back in line with the others.

She sat in the high-backed executive chair and opened the top drawer. As she rummaged through the man's supplies, she noticed at least a dozen specialty measuring devices, everything from odd-shaped metal rulers to digital gadgets. He probably used them on his fishing expeditions—gauging the size of his catch, she figured.

When she found what she was looking for—a pair of scissors—she took it out and put it on the desk, sliding it toward the picture frames, then got to her feet.

It took more than a couple of steps for her to arrive at the front of the spacious desk. She spun and leaned her backside against the corner of the surface, her eyes surveying the rest of the room.

Visions of other possible uses for the measuring tools in his desk flashed through her mind—all of them about the man's private area. The suddenness of the imagery sent her arms back for balance, knocking one of the pictures to the floor. Glass sprayed everywhere.

"Snap out of it, Tess," she said, sweeping the glass into a pile with her foot. She peered over her shoulder at the desk—the desk that would've belonged to her if she'd only said yes to the offer for the Director's job.

She grabbed the scissors and went over to his couch and cut off a strip of leather, before wrapping it around the wound in her leg. She cinched it tight, not knowing how bad the injury was, but at least she was able to walk, despite the pain.

Tess eyed the window, then hobbled over to it. She opened the lower panel and took a quick peek down at the street. There weren't any troops. Not like Dom had expected, only a few scattered trash dumpsters ready for their next scheduled pickup day.

Maybe the Russians found the persons they were looking for and moved on. She was certain the guy who had been chasing her would've stormed the office by now. Then again, the assumption might have only been wishful thinking.

Either way, she was thankful to still be alive. She made another sweep of the room for something to tie the rope to and make her way down. Yet there weren't any pipes or exposed beams. "Come on. Think."

Her eyes landed on the answer—the metal desk. It was old—like something you'd find at a secondhand store—and more importantly, heavy.

She moved the chair out of the way, then used all her weight to push the desk to the window. Its legs squeaked as it sputtered across the cement, creting a horrible vibration that darted up her arms.

Tess tied the rope from front to back using a square knot. The memory of her uncle teaching her how to tie knots on her tenth birthday was so vivid—it was a happy memory. A motivating you-better-stay-alive memory.

She crawled on top of the desk and slid her legs feet first into the opening of the window. She squeezed the rope, which felt sturdy, then glanced down at her bare hands. She dug her heels into the frame of the window to keep steady as she twisted around, scanning the room. "Think Tess, think." That's when a new idea hit her.

She untied the laces on her sneakers and slipped them off before peeling her socks free. Once her shoes were back on her feet and the laces tied, she slid her hands into the socks. "This just might work."

When she put the line down, the end spiraled on the floor next to her, raising another idea in her mind. She bent down and picked up the untied end—her hands working with speed to make three knots, one over top of the other. "Hope that's enough."

Tess climbed out of the window and dangled from the opening, feeling the strain of her own body weight in her arms. She'd been a training machine every day for the past six months, but it didn't seem to be helping, making her wonder if this escape plan was a good idea.

In the end, she didn't have a choice. If the Russian was still seeking her out, he must have heard her moving the desk. Hell, the entire block probably did.

"Just breathe and don't look down," she whispered before sucking in a deep breath and letting her grip fade. Gravity took over, dragging her downward with a build-up of speed, the heat in her hands escalating from the friction.

When she came to the end of the rope, the triple knot she'd tied slammed into her hands, almost ripping her arms out of their sockets.

She winced in pain. Then her head started to buzz as each breath quickened to the point that she thought she might hyperventilate. But she managed to hold on, thanks to the adrenaline pumping through her veins.

Tess looked up but the window was no longer in her view. Below her was the alley, a good twenty feet away. Too far to jump. Damn it, she needed more rope.

She eyed one of the dumpsters with its trash overflowing. It was at least ten feet beyond her position, nowhere close to a straight drop into it.

"No choice," she muttered, pulling her sneakers up and leveraging their soles against the brick wall with her legs.

Before she could move, she heard a male's voice call out from above. "Halt!"

When she peered up, she saw the soldier who'd shot her, leaning out of the window and looking down.

Tess pushed hard with her legs to catapult herself before he spotted her, aiming to the left. Her hands held steady as she twisted around in mid-flight, whipping her spine against the side of the building with a thud, knocking the air from her lungs.

She was now on the other side of the dumpster, sliding back across the wall to where she had just been.

Gunshots rang out from above in a rattling burst of fire. None of them hit her, but she could hear them buzz past her ear. It wouldn't be long before her luck ran out and his aim got better.

A second later, her sway on the rope brought the dumpster directly below her position. She closed her eyes and let go, screaming the entire way down.

CHAPTER 3

"Tess, can you hear me?" a voice said from the darkness, tapping her face with a light touch.

"Soldier, dumbwaiter, shooting," Tess said, as she started to come to, realizing she was on her back.

"Don't move. Looks like you hit your head pretty hard."

When she opened her eyes, she saw Dom staring back at her, wiping her head with a damp cloth.

Her heart leapt when she saw his gorgeous face. She forced down the desire to lure him closer for another kiss. "What happened?"

He soothed her chestnut brown waves with a gentle touch. "I found you in the street, bleeding from your head."

"What? How?"

"I don't know, but you were out cold."

A sequence of events flashed in the back of her mind. First, it was the window in the Director's office.

Then the rope around her waist. It finished with socks on her hands and her letting go and screaming as she fell.

Tess looked at her hands. No socks. She grunted, then reached behind her head and felt a bump the size of an avocado pit sticking out of her hair. "I must have hit the side of the dumpster. I don't remember anything after that."

"Somehow you must have crawled away. Pure panic mode, I'm sure."

She nodded, then wished she hadn't. "I guess instinct takes over when people are trying to kill you. Where am I?"

"I brought you to a friend's place. He's out front, keeping an eye on things."

"I need to get to the Embassy. I just wanna go home, Dom. Where it's safe. I can't handle this anymore. It's just too much."

"I'll get you there, but we need to take care of your injuries first."

Tess leaned up on one elbow and looked around the rectangle-shaped room. There was little else of interest to see other than the dingy cloth-covered couch she was on, its cushions caving beneath her back. No windows either, and only a small folding table with a computer plus an odd blue plastic chair in the corner, opposite from her.

One of the walls farthest to her right was stacked floor-to-ceiling with boxes of food stores, ammo, water bottles, and rifles—each of them labeled in Russian with red marker ink.

A shoulder-height cabinet with double doors along its front stood along the wall, surrounded by a heap of trash. Empty cans of soda and a few protein-drink jugs were the most prominent, plus a scattering of energy bar wrappers.

"You're safe here. No one knows about this place," Dom said.

A rush of wind blew past Tess, then the door slammed shut and someone stepped up behind Dom.

"Correction, nobody *knew* about this place, until now. Why didn't you take her to the lab?" a man asked as he leaned in. "You know they'll be sweeping the area. Only a matter of time."

Dom hung his head. "I told you before. She can't be anywhere near the lab. That's the next place they'll search. And believe me, she's not going to say anything."

"I'll hold you to that."

Dom's friend was at least six-foot-four, with almost no meat on his bones. His button-up camouflage shirt and dark khakis hung off him like a ten-year-old boy wearing his father's clothes. He wore a gray beard that looked as though it hadn't been washed or trimmed in years. Neither had his greasy mop of curly hair—it was everywhere all at once, sticking out in random directions.

His eyes were sharp and piercing despite his disheveled appearance, looking the part of both the predator and the prey.

Dom clapped his hand on the man's shoulder. "This is my old buddy, Cosmo."

Tess gave the stranger a thin smile. "Cosmo? Never met anyone with that name before."

"Precisely," Cosmo said in a firm tone. "And you still haven't."

She let her smile fade, then pointed at the boxes. "What's all the stuff for?"

"Need to be prepared."

"For what?"

His eyes widened as he looked at Dom. "Anything."

Cosmo took the cloth from Tess' head, then gave her a trio of pink and white pills and a bottle of water.

She hesitated, staring at the capsules in her hand. "What are these?"

"They'll help with the disorientation," Cosmo said. "My own special recipe."

Dom snatched the pills out of Tess' hand and turned on Cosmo. "What the hell are you doing? She's not a test subject."

Dom looked over his shoulder at Tess. "Sorry. Cosmo used to be a biochemist back in the day. Seems he hasn't kicked the habit."

Tess took a moment to calm down, her situation growing worse by the moment. First, she was hunted by and almost killed by the Russian military, then she'd jumped from a building into a trash bin, only to wake up and come face-to-face with a psycho named Cosmo who wanted to drug her. "Dom, we really need to go."

"Try and stand up," Dom said, taking her hand to help her up.

Tess let him leverage her to her feet. Just then a wave of nausea hit her stomach, sending a surge of bile up her throat. She leaned over, gagging, before vomit flew from her mouth.

Dom and Cosmo stumbled backward, kicking pieces from the trash pile across the room.

"I'm so sorry. Where are the towels? I'll clean it up," Tess said, wiping her chin on the sleeve of her shirt.

Cosmo ignored her request. "Possible concussion. My stuff might help." He shrugged.

"I'll be fine," she responded. "At least the dizziness is gone." She looked at her leg.

Cosmo didn't miss a beat. "The bullet only grazed you. I cleaned and dressed the wound. Best I could do for now."

Tess searched Cosmo's face, looking for a sign of his true intentions—was he a friend or the enemy? "I can't thank you enough, really. Won't you let me clean up the mess?"

Cosmo shook his head and brought his eyes around to Dom.

"What about those coats?" Dom asked him.

Cosmo sighed, then walked with heavy feet to the cabinet with double doors. He opened them and stood to one side, stroking his oily beard.

Nausea churned in Tess' stomach once again. She shifted her gaze to the ceiling and took a deep breath, somehow keeping the bile contained. When she looked back at Cosmo, she noticed he'd arranged the contents of the cabinet into sections.

The left cabinet was filled with camo-colored clothes. Hangers full of them. The right side was stuffed with folded street clothes—everything gray and drab, as if Cosmo had robbed a Goodwill store back in the States, only stealing the most depressing items.

He grabbed a pair of fur-lined coats and two Russian hats from the top shelf and tossed them at Dom.

"Thanks again," Tess said to Cosmo after they dressed and left the room.

Dom closed the door and led Tess down a hallway that smelled of mold. There were five other doors—all closed and in need of paint—with a single light bulb flickering overhead. A set of stairs met them at the end of the corridor, leading in only one direction.

Tess turned and headed down with Dom next to her. He wove his fingers through hers. She didn't acknowledge the advancement, afraid he would pull his hand away. She wanted his touch to mean more than just making her feel safe. "He's an interesting friend."

"You mean intense."

"Actually, I mean psychotic. But I didn't want to be rude, him being your friend and all."

"He's all right, just seen his share of hell along the way."

"What was up with him giving me those pills?"

"I don't know. Whatever they were could've been fine, but I don't need you trippin' out right now."

The tone of Dom's voice turned lower and less emotional when he spoke again, sounding like a different person. "As for the Embassy, we'll drive as close as we can, but we'll need to ditch the car and walk the rest of the way. Keep in mind, I'm not sure what the status is at the Embassy. We will have to assess the situation once we get there."

Tess nodded, pulling his hand to her chest and holding it tight for a few steps. Even though everything he suggested seemed logical, something nagged at her gut about his sudden magnitude of

46

knowledge, and his far better command of the English language.

Until now, all he'd ever been was one of her students. Just some good-looking Eastern European guy, who worked hard and was always there with a helping hand.

"Where's your car?" she asked when they reached the street.

Dom peered down the block for a moment, then turned to face the building, as if he were hiding his face.

Tess wondered why the sudden change of direction, until she saw them—a convoy of military vehicles driving at a snail's pace, with armed troops walking beside the vehicles, some breaking off to check cars and storefront windows. They looked to be about three blocks away.

She turned to match Dom's position, deciding to keep her face hidden as well. "They're looking for me, aren't they?"

"Not sure, but I can't be seen with you either way," he said, sliding a set of car keys from his hand into hers. "Take my car; it's the white sedan across the street. You need to head north for two miles, then turn west for one, then head south until you come to the road called Malyy Konyushkovskiy Pereulok."

"Isn't that the long way around? And what about your car?"

"Yes, but it's the safest path. Trust me," he said, blinking a few extra times. "There will be a shopping mall on your left. Look for the cafe sign next to the Ralph Lauren on the corner. Park in the garage, top level somewhere so I can find it later, then walk the rest of the way. Just keep your head down and don't talk to anyone."

Dom surveyed the convoy one last time, then turned and walked toward the alley in silence.

Tess stood frozen in place with her mouth agape. Dom never said goodbye, nor did he give her one last hug. He just left her standing there, alone—after spewing a few instructions and leaving her with a vehicle that looked older than she was.

It took a few seconds for her confusion to clear. Once it did, she thought through the plan and told her legs to get moving. Now.

The sedan wasn't far, needing only ten strides to reach it. She unlocked the car and slid into the driver's seat, fumbling with the keys until she found the one for the ignition.

She stuck it into the ignition, her eyes watching the action in the rearview mirror. The convoy was closer now, yet still two blocks away.

"Time to get out of here," she said, turning the key.

The engine whined but didn't start. She tried again and again and again—same thing. She slammed the steering wheel with her hands, wondering why Dom gave her keys to a dead car.

Tess glanced at the entrance to the alley to see if by some chance Dom was there. All she saw was the chipped pavement and a pair of brick walls.

The car was flooded for sure by now, she figured, her breaths growing shorter as she watched the military vehicles crawling ever closer in the mirror above her eyes.

Tess opened the door and slipped out and onto the sidewalk, keeping her movement natural and even, not wanting to catch anyone's attention. She pulled the hat low over her eyes, dropping her gaze to the ground as she traveled in the opposite direction of the convoy.

A few steps later, she entered the same alley where Dom had disappeared. The long passageway was empty—of people at least, with only random pieces of cardboard, plastic bottles, dumpsters, and broken glass visible. Dom must have taken off running once he made the corner. She sighed, knowing he was long gone.

As soon as she was sure she was out of sight, she broke into a sprint. It was at that moment when the throbbing in her leg began. Flesh wound or not, it was going to hurt. She'd give anything for an entire bottle of aspirin right about now.

Tess slowed her pace when she reached the far end of the alley, switching to a casual walk—a welcomed relief for the ache in her thigh—then she pulled the collar of her coat higher on her neck.

That's when she saw smoke billowing into the sky. It was on a path to where she knew the Embassy stood.

"Oh please, no," Tess said, trying to convince herself it was another building, even though the knot in her stomach screamed that it wasn't.

She wanted to run at full speed to find out, but she kept her pace measured, not just because of the wound in her leg, but because every decision she would make the rest of the way would need to be deliberate and precise if she hoped to make it to the Embassy alive.

Dom wanted her to take the long way around with the car, but now she was on foot. The smoke ahead marked the spot—the shortest path to the means of her escape, but it also marked the possible location of her death. So many variables. So little time.

Before her next step, a hand landed on her shoulder from behind, clamping down on her coat.

A scene of a man flashed in her mind—a faceless Russian soldier holding a gun aimed at her head.

"Where are you going?" a male's voice asked in Russian.

Tess spun with her hands high, expecting to see the end of a weapon. But that's not what she saw.

A man stood before her with a dirty face and torn clothes. His mouth drooled from a set of black teeth—at least the ones that weren't missing. He looked like a homeless jack-o-lantern as his hand moved to her arm, latching on with force.

Her plans changed from *woman of surrender* to *total ninja bitch* as she yanked her arm away in a flash of movement, knocking his grip loose. "Let go of me," she snapped in Russian.

He grabbed her again, this time with both hands. "Oh, feisty—I like that. Why don't we go have ourselves a little party, yes?"

"I don't think so," Tess said, flailing her arms, trying to squirm out of his grasp a second time. His two-handed grip never waned, not for a second, no matter how hard she struggled. That's when she let her body fall limp, giving in to his control, hoping he'd take the bait.

"That's better. I've got a special place we can go. It's right over here—"

When he turned to point, she brought her mouth down, chomping on the nearest finger. She sank her teeth in deep, feeling the skin above his middle knuckle break open and a flood of warmth enter her mouth. The metallic taste of his blood was disgusting, but she kept her teeth engaged as the man screamed in pain.

An instant later, he let go of her arm and lurched back to pull his finger free, then wrapped it under the edge of his coat. He backed away with eyes wide. "You bitch!"

"Come near me again and I'll bite the damn thing off," she said with a scowl, showing the man a mouthful of teeth—all of them pristine white and intact, not the gnarly mess he sported.

She knew she had the look of a crazy person, but that was the point—it's what her training had taught her.

He turned and stumbled into the alley, all the while mumbling something to himself in a fade of volume. His feet made a beeline for a stack of cardboard leaning against the wall, where he climbed under and disappeared.

She must have walked right by the boxes a minute ago, when her eyes were locked onto the smoke trail. "Come on, Tess. You have to stay focused."

She collected a wad of saliva on her tongue and spat it out, repeating the same process several times, hoping to rid herself of putrid taste, never mind whatever diseases he may have been carrying. No time to think about that. Got to move. Now.

"Head for the smoke, Tess. Just head for the smoke."

CHAPTER 4

The presence of military personnel became denser as Tess approached the area filling with smoke. There were trucks, men, and a whole slew of vehicles she didn't recognize, clogging up the streets.

She crouched behind a wall with a sign on the front of it that pointed the way to the Moscow Zoo. It wasn't easy to focus her thoughts, not with her legs feeling like Jell-O. Plus, she needed sleep. And a shower. At least the pain from the bullet wound hadn't gotten any worse.

The last few blocks took longer to navigate than she expected, because she had to slip from one doorway to the next, trying to stay out of sight.

She had no idea what she was doing, but one thing was for sure—she was alone. And everyone was her enemy now. Okay, so that was two things. She pinched the bridge of her nose. "I really need sleep."

Before she could pull her hand down, she heard a barrage of gunshots in the distance. It sounded like World War III had just started, snapping her out of her groggy state.

Just then, someone behind her cleared their throat and clamped down on her shoulder, again, making her flinch.

Tess thought it was the homeless man back for round two with his drool and rotting teeth, so she brought her fists up, ready to strike.

"Easy there. It's me," the man said, holding his arms out in a surrender position. It was Dom's weird biochemist friend, Cosmo.

She put her hands down and relaxed her stance.

Cosmo gave her an intense look. "Follow me if you want to live."

Tess hesitated a few beats to consider her options. There were only two she could come up with: sneak into the heart of the Russian military swarming the streets, or follow a man who'd patched her up and given her safe harbor for a short stretch. A strange man with a propensity to drug his guests.

If Dom had been with her, she could've bounced all this shit off him. No, if Dom had been with her, this situation wouldn't exist. Regardless, the answer was obvious—even though she hated the idea of either choice.

She nodded and followed Cosmo to the back of a building a block away. However, as soon as they cleared the next corner, Tess saw the eyes of a Russian soldier, pacing with his hands behind his back, looking irritated and in deep-think mode.

"No! No! No!" Tess said, holding her hands up in a stay-away-from-me pose.

"Here she is. The American," Cosmo said, pointing at Tess.

Tess turned and made a break for the street, but Cosmo flew forward and used an arm bar to stop her exit.

She reacted out of instinct, spinning and kneeing him in the crotch, just like she'd taught the young girls to do in her self-defense classes at the Center.

Cosmo folded over in a gasp with his hands on his groin, but the soldier was too quick. He locked a powerful grip on her wrist.

"You coming with me," the man said in broken English, folding her arm behind her back and marching her forward.

Tess weakened her stance and arched her spine, trying to lessen the stress on her arm. The pain was intense, making her wonder if her arm would break.

They didn't get ten steps before a loud ping echoed in the brisk air, ringing out from behind.

When the Russian soldier turned to look, so did Tess.

Dom stood a few feet away, holding a length of two-inch-wide black pipe in his hands. He hovered over the body of Cosmo, who lay motionless, with his forehead bleeding in spurts an inch above the right eye.

When the soldier's grip loosened, she reached up with her right hand and grabbed hold of his pinkie and pulled it hard to the side, making him yell out in pain.

She continued twisting his finger until his knees buckled, allowing her to slip free from his grasp.

The Russian went for the gun on his hip as Dom let out a guttural scream and charged him with the pipe held high.

When Tess saw the barrel of the pistol pointed at Dom, something inside of her took over. She jumped on the Russian's gun hand, knowing that if he brought the weapon up and fired, Dom would be dead.

The soldier's hand flung to the side under the weight of her body, and did so only a split second before he pulled the trigger. An ear-splitting gunshot rang out, creating a high-pitched ringing sound that tore into her eardrums.

She pulled on the Russian's arm, hoping to keep her leverage in place, but he was too strong and shook her off.

An instant later, his other arm came around and delivered a fist to the side of her head, sending her flopping to the ground, her head spinning from vertigo.

Another loud ping resonated from the pipe before the clatter of a gun hitting the pavement. When Tess looked through the dizziness, she saw Dom bring the pipe over his head, then swing it down at the skull of the Russian, who was already bleeding and bent down on one knee.

The pipe made contact again, this time caving in the back of the Russian's head. The man fell hard, landing headfirst on the asphalt.

Dom brought the pipe up again, preparing to deliver another strike.

"Dom! Stop!" Tess screamed, seeing the soldier defenseless.

Dom froze with his hands over his head. "I have to, Tess. They'll never stop coming for you."

"Please, don't. We just need to leave."

He ignored her plea and brought the pipe down. It crushed the soldier's head, making Tess gasp in horror as some of the man's brain matter seeped out, creating a heap of clotted tissue.

Dom's face looked numb as he walked over to Cosmo and did the same, whacking the guy's skull several times until his body stopped twitching.

When he was done, Dom held his eyes on his lifeless friend and spoke through clenched teeth. "You picked the wrong side, Boris."

Tess couldn't believe what she'd just witnessed. Whoever this pipe-wielding man was, he was not the Dom she thought she knew. A cold-blooded killer? Never. But the way he swung that pipe told her he'd killed before. He was too good at it.

"How could you do that?" Tess asked, rubbing the side of her head as her unsteadiness waned.

"That soldier would have interrogated, tortured, and killed you. You saw what they did at the Center."

"I know, but—" Tess said, her mind running dry of words. Her entire body ached. She bent over with her hands on her knees and her head swimming with exhaustion.

Part of her wanted to scream at Dom for killing two men, one being his friend Cosmo, or Boris, or whatever his real name was. But then again, Dom had just saved her from the Russians. Not once, but twice. There were no words for any of this. "Just get me out of here. Please."

"This way," Dom said, pointing in the direction of the smoke filling the sky.

"No, there are too many. I've seen them. They're everywhere."

"I know a better way, but you need to trust me."

She peered into his eyes for a beat, then at his hand holding the pipe. "That's a big ask at the moment."

"Right, sorry," he said, tossing the weapon into the corner. It landed next to a stack of flattened cardboard boxes. "I'm sorry you had to see any of that."

"Who are you? Really?"

"I'm just a guy who is helping a really nice girl," Dom said, his tone condescending.

She swore she'd heard that line in some old Hollywood movie. As if killing two men and tossing aside the murder weapon was no big deal, because he was just *helping* a nice girl.

"Why didn't you take my car?" he asked.

"Because it wouldn't start. I had to do something. They were getting close."

"Yeah, it does that sometimes."

"You just left me there. Alone. Why would you do that?"

"Tess, there are things you don't know about me."

"I get that. Lots of things, apparently."

"But none of that matters now. We need to get you to the Embassy. Before it's too late."

"What does that mean, exactly?"

"It means this isn't over. Not by a long shot. Your people are evacuating. You need to as well."

Tess stared him down, wondering who was really hiding behind all that boyish charm and pent-up anger that just crushed heads.

It was clear she didn't know the first thing about her long-time friend. There were loads of questions that needed to be asked, but she knew he wouldn't answer them—and if he did, would he tell the truth?

In the end, Dom was right, it didn't matter. All she wanted was to go home. To the States. Dom was her one and only choice, even if she didn't know who he was anymore. "Fine, just get me there. I'm so tired I can hardly stand."

He shifted into stealth mode as they made their way like a pair of covert spies, using doorways, trees, benches, cars, and walls for cover, maneuvering them around the turmoil with precision.

It was clear Dom was no innocent, flirtatious kid who'd been taking her courses for months, with the hope of scoring with her. Nor was he a menial lab technician, stuck in a job that he hated. He was someone else entirely. He had training. Skills. Only an idiot wouldn't be able to see it.

Despite the contradictions, she was afraid to ask him about it. In truth, she didn't want to know. None of it would matter anyway, not once she was safe in American hands and on her way home.

Yet that meant she'd never see Dom again. Not after today. That fact was both comforting and painful at the same time.

When they stopped behind a retaining wall near a park, she reached out and squeezed his arm. "Dom," she whispered. "I don't know if I can do this. I'm so scared."

Dom glanced around, his eyes wide and darting from point to point. Then he leaned in and pulled her close. "It's all right. I've got you."

The instant her cheek felt the warmth of his breath, she couldn't stop her desire to kiss him. Her lips went to his, pressing softly.

At first Dom didn't respond, then he did, weaving his fingers through her hair, sending a tingle across her body. He wrapped an arm around her waist, sliding her beneath him as their kiss continued.

Dom was the first to let his breathing slow, bringing their intimate moment to an end.

"Thank you for saving my life," she said, her mouth lingering next to his.

"No need to thank me. I'd save you a million times over. But things are different now and—"

She put a finger to his mouth and nodded.

Again, Dom was right, things were different now. Not just with the two of them, but with the world. Everyone had gone insane. Dom, the Russians, and even her. She'd gotten shot, jumped out of a window, and even threw herself on a soldier's gun and lived to tell about it. Only a crazy person would do that.

It was at that moment she realized what Dom was trying to tell her, in his own gentle way. When your entire world is turned inside out, there's no time for love affairs. Or sanity. Or logic, for that matter.

It's simply time to act.

Or die.

CHAPTER 5

When they made it to the street bordering the back of the Embassy, Tess knelt next to Dom, nestling in shoulder to shoulder. He picked her hand up and intertwined his fingers with hers. She knew what these gestures meant now. It wasn't about love or romance. It was about safety, nothing more. Regardless, it felt comforting and she relished it.

His hand was strong and wide, smothering hers like a warm blanket. Sometimes, the simplest touch from another human being can change your outlook on everything. Even more so when your world is descending into a state of anarchy.

Her mind flashed to the first time she'd seen this area of town. The trees stood green and plentiful, not anything like the frozen wasteland she had expected when she arrived several years earlier.

When she first decided to take the job in Moscow, she heard all of the rumors about what she was walking into, all of them scary and under military control, but none of them turned out to be real—until now.

This was the very nightmare she'd always feared. Except for Dom—he was the only bright light.

Dom leaned forward, pulling Tess with him and shaking her from her thoughts. He stared at something or someone, so she followed his line of sight to see what it was—a burst of people running out of the back of the Embassy. Three to be exact, one woman and two men—one of the males carrying a briefcase.

"Are those Embassy employees?" she asked in a whisper.

A second later, four men appeared from the back of building, wearing camo gear and helmets, each walking backwards with their rifles held high and aimed back at the door they'd just exited.

Dom nodded. "And those are Marines. Probably stationed there."

A second later, the windows above the Marines exploded in a fury, as the building fell victim to numerous fires inside.

Tess ducked when a barrage of gunshots blared to the right of them, but Dom held firm. The

Marines protecting the civilians didn't react either. Nor did they fire. They just kept moving in reverse, sweeping their rifles from side to side to cover the others.

"Don't worry. The fight is on the other side of the building," he said.

When Dom turned to her, he released her hand and pointed at the Embassy employees scurrying across the street. "You need to go with them. They're heading to a transport plane."

"How do you know that?"

"It's standard evacuation procedure."

She furrowed her brow. "Tell me how you know all this."

"It's the only option they have. Now go. Before it's too late."

"No. I'm not leaving you here. It's not safe. Not after everything you've done. You need to come with me and ask for asylum. I'll tell them how you saved me."

"No Tess, I can't."

She balled his shirt sleeve in her hand. "Yes, you can. My uncle is a Senator. They'll have to listen. I promise."

Jo Nash, Jay J. Falconer, M.L. Banner

Dom freed himself and pushed her away with a gentle but firm force. "There isn't time to debate this. Go, Tess. Now. Get out of here. Those Marines will protect you in ways I can't."

Tess held for a beat, then got up and dissolved into tears as she ran. Thank God her body was on autopilot, her legs taking her down the sharp incline and across the pavement toward a cement barrier on the right. A four-door vehicle sat a few feet in front of it.

She caught up to the employees as they got into the black sedan, the woman sliding into the front passenger seat, while the two men with the briefcase got in the back. Someone with dark hair was already in the driver's seat.

"Wait! Wait for me!" Tess said, waving her arms.

The driver leaned out of the car door and scrunched his bushy eyebrows, as if he were trying to figure out who she was yelling at.

Tess sucked in an extra breath before she reached them, her lungs struggling for air. "Please, I'm an American. My uncle is a Senator. You have to help me. Please!"

"Tess? Tess Wainwright?" the woman in the front seat asked after she rolled down the window.

"Yes," Tess said in a breathy voice, wondering how the woman knew her name.

"We've been hoping you'd show up. Hop in."

Tess got in and shoved herself against the two men in the back seat. The driver sped off just as she reached back and closed the door.

"Where are we going?" Tess asked the woman in the front, thinking of Dom's insistence of protocol.

"The International Science and Technology lab."

"Not anymore," the driver said, his tone sharp. "Plans have changed."

Their answers didn't help in the least. In fact, they added to her nervousness, as she wondered if Dom had been making up his tactical expertise as he went along. If he had, it was probably to keep her calm and submissive, she decided.

Tess spun to look out the back window as the car drove ahead.

Dom was there among the trees, right where she'd left him, standing tall with his hands in his front pockets. Always confident. Always vigilant. Even so, she had the feeling he was now alone and vulnerable, making her heart ache deep in her chest.

If the Russians ever found out what he'd done for her, it wouldn't go well for him. Their mission wouldn't only be to kill every American, but to kill him and those who helped any American escape.

When Dom's face disappeared from view, Tess turned and slid back into the seat. She wiped the tears from her cheeks, then leaned her head back, taking a moment to steady herself.

That's when her mind filled with a single question. One she didn't want to know the answer to, but one she had to ask. "Did anyone else make it out?"

The gray-haired woman spun her neck and looked back. "I'm not a hundred percent sure, but as far as the Embassy staff is concerned, we're it. They hit us before we knew what happened. First with some rockets, then they swarmed the gate."

"We're being followed," the driver said in a clipped tone, his eyes alternating between the road ahead and the mirror above.

Tess turned to see two Russian military vehicles gaining on them from behind. They weren't Jeeps exactly, or Humvees. They were something in between, though Tess wasn't well versed in different types of military vehicles. All she knew was they looked well-armed and were closing fast.

"Step on it, Stan!" the woman said to the driver, who sported a black mustache and greasy hair that had been slicked back over his ears, plus a pair of mirrored sunglasses sitting on top of his head. All that was missing was his leisure suit and bellbottom pants—as if he'd stepped right out of an old 70s TV show.

Stan floored the gas pedal, but the military vehicles matched their speed, then began to overtake them, working their way forward and spreading out from each other.

Her gut twisted, telling her that the Russians were going to try and force the car off the road, then take them hostage.

Then her logic chimed in, screaming something different. All day, they'd had a singular focus—gun everyone down. Nothing else.

Tess brought her eyes to the back of the Stan's head. "Why aren't they shooting at us?"

"And you're complaining?" he snapped before slamming on the brakes, sending the military vehicles into a swerving skid behind them.

When the sedan came to a stop, Tess watched Stan twist his body forward and thrust his hand down, somewhere below the seat. When his hand came back up, a black, square-looking pistol was in his fingers. He gave it to the woman. "You shoot, Carol, while I drive. Can't do both."

Carol took the gun, but held it by the grip with only the tips of her fingers, as if it were a stinky fish. "I can't shoot this thing."

"Give it to me," Tess said, cutting her off. She leaned forward and snatched the gun, not knowing where her sudden bravery was coming from. It was as if she were channeling Dom in some cosmic way. "What do I do?"

"Just aim and pull the trigger. It's not that hard," Stan said, folding a piece of gum onto his tongue, then putting the car in reverse and beginning to accelerate. "Do it now, before they *do* open fire and kill us all. Just try not to shoot me while you're at it."

Tess sat on the edge of the seat and rolled down the side window, then leaned out with the gun in her hand, pointing it at the trucks in pursuit.

She squeezed the trigger a bunch of times, firing without much of an aim, praying she'd hit something as the gun recoiled after each shot. She pulled her arm back in with her ears ringing. "How many bullets are there?"

"The mag holds ten," Stan answered with his head spun around and looking past Tess as he drove in reverse. "You'll know when it's empty. The slide will lock open."

He remained in that position with his foot planted on the gas for several hundred feet, then he turned the wheel hard, putting the car in drive and gunning it forward, the tires screeching the entire way.

Carol had one hand on the dash and the other one on the glass next to her, her fingers turning white as she tried to steady herself.

The other two passengers on the bench seat next to Tess had their faces down by their knees and hands together behind their heads. One of them had the black briefcase lodged between their feet.

"Hey you, ignore them and shoot!" Stan said to Tess, his voice gruff. His eyes flared in the rearview mirror as his hands worked the steering wheel.

"Right, on it," Tess answered as Stan started weaving the car in a zigzag pattern.

Tess spun in her seat, then leaned out of the window with the gun pointed behind them.

Right before she fired, one of the Russian trucks slammed into their rear bumper. The gun tipped to the side, sending the bullet barreling into a random parked car. She rocketed backward, her ribcage smashing into the door frame.

"Oh no you don't," Tess said after a wince, wedging her torso between the driver's seat and the car door to keep her balance. She fired again, the round glancing off the front grille with a spark. "Come on!"

Two more rounds found their way to the windshield of the ramming vehicle, but it didn't slow down or veer off, continuing the chase.

As she prepared to click off another shot, the truck rammed them again. This time she was ready, bracing herself so the force wouldn't send her into the frame as hard.

She aimed for the closest tire and fired, but her hand wobbled and she missed.

"Why aren't you shooting?" Stan asked, his voice rising above the howl of wind through the window.

Tess held up the pistol, its slide locked open. "Out of bullets. Sorry, I tried."

"And you hit nothing? Damn it," he said, turning the wheel hard to the left. Everyone inside the car flew to the side, slamming into each other.

Tess righted herself. "How much farther?"

Stan glanced in the mirror. "Almost there."

Tess whipped her head around in time to see the Russians increasing their speed with a roar of their engines. "Here they come again."

"Hold on," he said, slamming on the brakes and spinning the wheel hard to take the next turn, with a burst of acceleration behind it. He sent the car up on two wheels as he accelerated, propelling them onto a dirt road.

The first Russian truck flew past them on the previous straightaway, disappearing from view. Now only one Russian vehicle remained on their tail, taking the same turn they'd just made, only not as fast.

Tess didn't know Stan at all, but she knew one thing for sure—he could drive, righting the car as it started to fishtail.

"Everyone put your heads down. Now!" he said.

Tess glanced over at the two guys next to her. Not only had they sat in silence the entire trip, but they were still folded over in what she assumed was their version of crash mode.

When Tess looked beyond the hood, she saw what Stan was focused on—a huge chain link fence dead ahead, with razor wire in a circular pattern across the top of it.

Two all-white semi-tractor trailer rigs stood on either side of the road, with a litany of armed troops positioned on top of them, plus a few crouched on one knee in front. They appeared to be protecting a sea of cement beyond the fence, where a trio of industrial buildings sat waiting in the distance.

"Are those Russians?" Tess asked, her heart pounding in her ears.

"No, they're ours. They knew we were coming. Put your head down."

"But how? We could be anyone."

"Got it covered," he said, honking the horn in three long blasts, then two short and finishing with one long.

The troops manning the semi-trucks lowered their weapons a few degrees, then black smoke started to rise from the exhaust pipes on the semi-trucks in strong, haphazard puffs.

"Ramming speed!"

"Why don't they just open the gate?" Tess asked.

Stan looked at her in the mirror. "Do you see one anywhere?"

"No, but—"

"This isn't a real business. It's owned by the CIA. Now. Put. Your. Head. Down."

After they flew past the troops and drove between the trucks, the semis started to close together.

Tess bent down and covered her head when they approached the fence at top speed. The car lurched from the impact, sending her off balance when Stan corrected with the wheel.

The impact made a wicked metallic sound. Some of the fence bounced off the hood, tearing at the paint, while another section must have gotten hung up on something as it was being dragged behind the car, making a loud and distinct clanking sound.

"Damn it! I swallowed my gum," Tess heard Stan mumble from the front seat.

The CIA troops opened fire at the Russians just as Stan took them left in a slow turn. The Russians must have started shooting back because the intensity of the gunfight seemed to triple.

When she brought her head up, she realized they had made it all the way around the side of the leftmost warehouse and to its rear, where a blue and gray helicopter waited with blades spinning. There were letters stenciled on the craft in Russian.

If Tess' Russian to English conversion was correct, the lettering said *International Science and Technology Laboratories Inc*. The same place Carol had mentioned when Tess asked where they were headed.

"There's our ride," Stan said, bringing the car to a stop. Everyone threw the doors open and rushed the helicopter in a frenzy.

The side door to the chopper slid open, giving Tess a direct view of a man crouched inside. He wore a padded headset, sunglasses, and a flight jumpsuit—

gray in color with no markings, nametags, or patches on it.

He put out his palm, helping Carol in first. The man with the briefcase went into the airship next, then Tess and the other man hopped in, with Stan filing in last.

The instant the door slammed shut, the pilot took off in a roar of the engine. The sound was overwhelming, making Tess' eardrums hurt. She covered her ears, but the noise was still getting through.

The man in the jumpsuit tapped her on the shoulder and gave her one of the five headsets now in his hands. Tess didn't need to be told twice, putting the headset over her ears, then adjusting the microphone, following his hand instructions to do so.

The others received a headset, too, each covering their ears and adjusting their mics as well.

"Buckle up, folks. This might be a rough ride," a woman's voice said over the cockpit radio, blasting her confidence into the padded speakers covering their ears. Tess assumed the voice was the pilot's.

Tess found the seatbelt tucked along the back of the seat and slipped it on before letting out a long exhale she'd been holding. She couldn't remember when she took in that breath, but it must've been somewhere on this side of the fence, after they'd smashed through it.

The ground below her disappeared in less than a minute as they climbed into the sky, tilting upward at a steep angle. The female pilot flew like Stan drove, keeping Tess' hands glued to the seat, her fingers digging into the fabric.

At least she was safe. For now, anyway, hoping she was past the worst of it.

CHAPTER 6

Ben Wainwright parked his Jeep next to an unknown sedan sitting in front of his father's house, its tailpipe leaking exhaust into the crisp morning air.

It wasn't the presence of a vehicle he didn't recognize that gave him pause, it was the fact that it was a luxury Cadillac. Unexpected visitors almost always drove a black SUV with tinted windows, not a chromed-out white sedan with fancy rims and a suite of antennas.

Either way, he figured it was another Senator from Washington, here to work a deal with his dad or call in a long-standing political favor. Deals are usually the first order of the day for any Senator, and his father was no different.

Ben waited to see if the driver of the Caddy would signal for him to move his Jeep, wanting to keep the area clear in proximity.

When the man behind the wheel looked over at Ben, he didn't give any sort of signal, only leaning toward the passenger seat, then sitting upright with a cell phone to his ear.

Ben turned to the German Shepherd sitting in the back seat. "Come on Wilma, let's see who's visiting Dad today." He opened the back door and reached inside. "Let's go," he said, clipping a leash to the dog's collar before she hopped to the ground.

He watched Wilma wind from side to side, smelling the grass and bushes as they made their way up the manicured walkway. Each shrub had been trimmed into the shape of an different animal, leaving Ben to wonder how long it took Manny and his crew to complete the task each week.

Ben snapped his head up when the front door flew open and two men stormed out and hurried down the steps.

The Shepherd went ballistic, barking and leaping at the men.

An obese man in a business suit stepped behind another well-dressed guy who, Ben figured, must've been his bodyguard, because he was at least six-four with bulging muscles that gave him the appearance of not having a neck.

"Hey, who are you?" Ben asked.

Muscle man grabbed the obese guy by the arm and escorted him to the car in a rush, then pushed him into the backseat.

Ben's stomach churned, looking back at the front door, then bringing his eyes forward again to the Caddy peeling out of the driveway. "What the hell is going on?"

He sprinted into the house and up the stairs with Wilma at his side, stopping at the door to his father's study. He knocked four times with a heavy fist. "Dad?"

There was no answer.

He pounded at the door again. "Dad, are you okay?"

More silence.

Ben turned the knob and pushed the door open to find his father sitting at his desk, with one hand digging into a glass bowl of M&Ms, and the other keeping a cell phone to his ear.

"You withheld information from me, Alan! There is no *dealing* with Russia. They sent people to my house, for Heaven's sake!" Edgar Wainwright said before tossing some candy into his mouth. He looked up at Ben standing in the doorway. "I need to call you back." He put his phone in his shirt pocket and attempted to stand, wrapping an arm around his torso.

Ben rushed to the far side of the desk and held the rolling executive chair steady as his father pushed to his feet in a grimace, his mouth still in chew mode.

"Are you okay?" Ben asked, wondering how anyone could eat chocolate while they were in such obvious pain.

Edgar put his hand on Ben's chest, patting it with a soft touch. "I'm fine. I'm fine, it's nothing."

"What the hell happened?"

"Nothing you need to worry about."

"I disagree. You need to—"

Before Ben could finish his sentence, his dad's cell phone rang.

Edgar yanked it out of his pocket, then squinted at the screen. "I need to take this."

Ben latched onto his father's arm. "No, what you need to do is go to the hospital."

"I told you before, I'm fine. It's nothing," Edgar said, wincing again as his lungs fought for more air. "Now go wait for me in the hallway."

Ben stood with frozen feet, not wanting to leave.

"I'm not going to say it again. Wait for me outside. I have to take this call. It's important."

Ben let go and stormed across the floor, leaving the office in a huff. He slammed the door behind him, whispering to Wilma, who was waiting in the hall with a wagging tail. "Like it's really gonna matter. I can hear everything he says through the door."

He bent down and scratched Wilma between the ears, debating if he should eavesdrop or not. It wouldn't be the first time and given the fact that two guys just stormed out of the house and his father was in pain, it seemed like the right thing to do.

Wilma arched her back as Ben ran his fingers through her fur. "If those guys hurt Dad, I should've let you have a piece of them. Huh, girl?"

Ben leaned in close to the door, hearing his father's voice grow louder.

"Do whatever you have to, Colonel. No excuses. Just get it done. I want her out of Russia in one piece. Is that clear? She's my only niece and I want her home, now!"

Ben heard a thud, then the shattering of what sounded like glass.

"To hell with this," Ben told Wilma as he pushed the door open with a two-arm shove, sending it crashing into the wall on the other side. He ran in, seeing the candy bowl shattered across the floor with M&Ms everywhere.

"Dad, you okay?"

"I'm fine. I told you to wait outside."

"I thought you passed out or something."

"No. Just wishing people would do their damn jobs, like I tell them to do."

"I heard what you said to that Colonel. Is something wrong with Tess?"

"I really wish you'd respect my privacy, son. Listening in is a breach of national security."

"Like who's gonna know?"

"I will. So will you. Secrets need to be kept secret, no matter what. Even with family members."

"I get that, but you still haven't answered me. What the hell is going on? What about Tess?"

"She's fine."

"Doesn't sound like it to me. You were yelling at that guy to get her out of Russia. Did something happen?"

"There was an incident and she's being flown home. That's all I can tell you," Edgar said, walking to the front of his desk. He stopped to sweep the shards of glass into a pile with his foot. "Get me a broom and a dust pan, will ya? And maybe a vacuum, if we have one."

Ben ignored the request, knowing the maid would clean it up. His dad was just trying to change the subject. "When will she be home?"

"I'm waiting on that information," Edgar said, continuing to concentrate on the mess on the floor.

"What kind of incident?"

"The kind I'm not able to discuss."

"Because it has to do with Russia, right?" Ben asked, his voice edging higher. "Those guys that were here—are they after Tess? Are we in some sort of trouble?"

Edgar's eyes locked onto his. "Trust me, everything is fine. Those men are not after Tess. Now, you need to calm down. Everything's being handled."

"Don't tell me to calm down. I know something's wrong. Why don't you ever answer my questions?"

Edgar stared at him for a moment, then sighed. "You know why, son. It's for your safety. And the good of this country."

"Yeah, right. Whatever, I'm done," Ben snapped, turning for the door. He'd hit this same brick wall before with his father and knew it was a waste of breath. Stubborn should have been his father's middle name. That and cryptic asshole. "I have a training job in Vegas. You know how to reach me, assuming you're not dying in a hospital somewhere."

"Have a good trip. Stay safe."

Ben stopped and turned in the doorway. "Look, I know you won't listen to me, but try to go to the hospital, if you can. Those ribs might be broken and they can get a lot worse, if you don't get help."

"Don't worry about me. Your old man knows how to take care of himself."

With that, Ben spun and grabbed Wilma's leash and ran down the stairs, stopping at the front door. He could feel a pair of eyes on his back. He grabbed the knob and opened the front door before turning and peering up the stairs.

His father stood at the top of the landing with his hands on his hips—his lips silent.

Ben waited a few beats, then shrugged before stepping outside and closing the door behind him. He walked to his Jeep and tucked Wilma into the back seat, then stood and took his phone out from his jean pocket. His fingers worked the buttons that controlled the list of pre-programmed numbers, stopping at the third one on the list.

He pressed the key labeled CALL and waited for an answer. Four rings ticked by before a voicemail message greeted him. "Hey, this is Tess. You know what to do at the beep. Ciao."

Jo Nash, Jay J. Falconer, M.L. Banner

CHAPTER 7

"Last stop to refuel. You know the drill, blindfolds everyone," the helicopter pilot said, her tone much too cheery.

Tess winced at the now familiar crackle of the headset as it beat against her eardrums. Granted, she'd take the noise over the pain she'd experienced when she first climbed on board, but she was almost done with all this insanity. Done with helicopter rides. Done with having to be blindfolded because civilians aren't allowed to see secret CIA sites. Done being chased by men with rifles who wanted to kill her. Done watching innocent people get mowed down without mercy.

She pulled the blindfold over her eyes, thankful this would be the last time. When the chopper started its rapid descent, her stomach dropped, leaving her with a level of queasiness she'd never felt before.

It was all she could do not to vomit on the man in the flight suit sitting across from her.

A few minutes later, the skids on the helicopter touched the ground. She waited until the engine faded to a low whine, then grew quiet as the clomp of boot-steps approached them.

It's a surreal kind of experience when you're forced to be blind and your heartbeat is approaching critical levels. Now that the roar of the helicopter wasn't pounding at her ears, Tess could hear far more detail coming from the world around her.

First, the shuffling of paper, which she assumed was the pilot going through her paperwork. Then Carol clearing her throat before she whispered something to Stan, who continued to chomp his gum like a madman. And per usual, not a peep from the guy with the briefcase or his counterpart, both a couple of mute robots.

"Hurry it up already," Carol said, with a hint of a wobble in her voice. Maybe she was just as anxious as Tess to finish the this leg of the journey. Get it over and done with, then make it back home.

Engine fumes seeped into the cabin, the smell scratching at Tess' throat. She coughed into her hand, then heard a series of clicks, bumps and muffled voices.

"You okay over there?" Stan asked her.

"Uh, yeah. Thanks. Just about ready to rip this blindfold off."

Stan snorted. "I hear ya. Sounds like they're just about done."

Stan, nor anyone else for that matter, had spoken to her the entire trip. Tess jumped on the opportunity, needing him to answer some questions that she couldn't hold back. "What happened in Moscow? I mean—"

"Not here, Tess. Wait—"

Before Stan could finish his sentence, gunfire could be heard in the distance. Tess flinched in her seat when someone pounded on the side of the helicopter.

"Go, go, go!" a male's voice said.

She slipped her headset on, as the blades whirred to life. They peeled off the ground moments later, tipping forward and to the side as the engine roared to life.

The deafening blast of an explosion penetrated her hearing protection, the reverberating boom bouncing off the glass and vibrating the seats.

"Screw this," Tess said, before tearing the black piece of cotton from her eyes, then peering out of the side of the craft. The other travelers did the same.

Tess gasped when she saw ant-sized people far below, bolting away from the fire consuming the back of the building. Others lay on the ground—none of them moving.

"Damn terrorists," Stan said in an even voice, running his fingers over his mustache.

No one responded.

Tess stared down at the scene until it was only a blob of red and brown—all run together in a mix of insanity.

"You may remove your blindfolds," the pilot said, her once-bubbly tone now somber.

Tess, Carol, and Stan turned toward the man in the gray uniform to find he had his eyes on them.

Carol started to speak, probably to explain why they'd broken the blindfold rule before the pilot told them it was okay to do so, but stopped when he lifted one of his hands in a halt motion. The sides of his mouth drooped as his gaze dropped, his eyes filled with tears and running into a long stare.

Tess put her hand on his knee, squeezing in support. She wanted to say something to help comfort him, but her mouth came up empty.

"How are you two holding up?" Stan asked the two men who never seemed to speak. The briefcase guy shrugged and the other man only sighed, neither adding any words in response.

Tess decided to call them The Silent Brothers, their lack of communication skills adding to her anxiety. She thought about checking to see if their tongues had been cut out, maybe by someone in the CIA, to guard against divulging what was being carried in the black briefcase. A morbid thought to be sure, but it was not out of the realm of possibility.

As she eyed the briefcase, a new idea hit her, taking the air out of her chest.

What if the contents of that pillow-sized container were the reason for everything that had just happened in Russia? The killings. The car chase. Their narrow escape.

She sucked in two more breaths, holding each for a three-count before letting it go. The moment they landed in Turkey, she planned to start asking questions.

If the Embassy crew wouldn't help, then she'd call her uncle, the Senator, and have him obtain the answers.

CHAPTER 8

"Hallelujah," Tess said, raising her hands in celebration as the U.S. Air Base in Turkey came into view. It looked like a mirage fluttering in the distance—complete with American servicemen, transport planes, and the pride-inducing red, white and blue of the American flag.

"When we exit the helicopter—" Carol said.

"—just follow me," Stan said, interrupting her comment. "We need to see the Colonel." He rammed another stick of gum into his mouth. Spearmint by the smell of it.

Stan made an odd twitch with his head, jostling the mirrored sunglasses that had become a permanent fixture on top of his head. The shades slid down, hands-free, and landed in place on his nose, making Tess wonder how many times he'd practiced that move.

Once they landed and the rotors stopped spinning, the man in the flight suit collected the

97

headset from each passenger, nodding in appreciation as everyone slid toward the exit door of the craft.

Tess wanted to ask him about the explosions at the last CIA site, but held her tongue as she hopped out. He, like the pilot and the rest of her crew, were not the people she needed to question. They were only the tools of their escape—the facilitators—not the brains behind the evacuation. Someone else was in charge and needed to help her understand what was going on and why.

When the soles of her shoes touched the ground, she thought about bending down and kissing the asphalt, never wanting to take another chopper ride for the rest of her life. But the surface looked disgusting, mostly grime and grease and a few cigarette butts.

She brought her eyes up and spotted three transport planes parked on the tarmac. "Is that how we're flying home?"

"That's up to Colonel Tanner," Stan answered, as he guided them toward the entry door of the domed building in front of them.

Stan pointed and let out a swooping whistle twenty yards later. "Would you look at that? An F-35?

Now that's what I call a true macho machine. Damn, talk about raw power."

Everyone turned to take in the view of three sleek, black and silver jets lined up in a row. She had to admit, it was an impressive sight.

Tess followed behind the Silent Brothers, wondering if they were going to hand the case to the Colonel. They were an odd pair, but both seemed confident in their duty as they walked with purpose, neither of them acting the least bit nervous during the evacuation.

Once inside, an attractive brunette beelined out from behind a desk and stood in front of Tess, her Air Force uniform tight and shoulders square. Her hair was tied into a neat bun and matched the precision she'd shown in applying her makeup.

If someone had asked Tess to describe the female Airman, the term she would have used was perfection. Not a blemish on her skin. Even her teeth were spotless, and there wasn't a single tooth she could see that was out of alignment. Her curves and fitness were evident as well, the woman towering over Tess by at least a foot.

"Ms. Wainwright?" the brunette asked, her badge stenciled with the name Clayborn.

"Yes?"

"Follow me, please," Clayborn said with her arm outstretched, guiding Tess to separate from the group.

When Tess looked back, she noticed Stan, Carol, and the Silent Brothers had been split up from each other and led off in different directions. She could hear Stan saying something about "need to see the Colonel, pronto."

"So much for grilling them about the briefcase," Tess said, keeping her voice low.

"Pardon me?" Clayborn asked.

"Nothing, sorry, just talking to myself."

They made their way through the crowded administrative area and across a mirror-polished floor, taking the hallway that ran to the right. Once they made it to the door at the end, Clayborn held it open for Tess to step through.

The name *Colonel Bret W. Tanner* was printed on the brass nameplate that had been affixed to the middle of the door with screws.

Clayborn closed the door, then moved to the side and stood in perfect form along the back wall.

The Colonel's stark office reminded Tess of her uncle's study in Bell Hill, Washington—everything in its place, yet somehow warm and inviting—right down to a bowl of mints, instead of M&Ms, on the cherry desk.

It may have been all the stained woodwork that gave the space its charm, Tess having expected only an ancient metallic desk and drab concrete walls.

Tess sat in silence for about forty-five minutes with Clayborn hovering nearby, when a man appeared through the door. The sudden burst of noise made Tess flinch in the chair, having almost fallen asleep in the quiet of the room

"Wait outside, Airman," the man said to Clayborn. His ID badge listed his last name as Tanner.

"Yes, Colonel," she responded in a crisp voice, leaving the room in a rush of air.

Tanner plucked a piece of candy from the bowl before sitting down, then tipped the container in Tess' direction.

"No, thank you," she replied, wondering if they were going to be offered any real food to eat. Her stomach was beyond empty, making rumbling sounds as if to say she was poor and desperate.

"I spoke with Senator Wainwright. You're one lucky lady."

Tess wasn't sure how being chased at gunpoint and almost dying several times was lucky, but she chose not to debate the man. "Does he know I'm here—that I'm safe? That I made it out of Moscow?"

"Yes ma'am, I sent word the moment you arrived. And again yes, your uncle is aware you made it out of Russia, because he's the reason you made it out in the first place. We'll be flying you home to the States shortly."

"When?"

"As soon as we clear the flight. Waiting for orders to come through now. Shouldn't be long. In the meantime, I'd like you to pay a visit to our staff physician. Have her do a once-over to make sure you're shipshape and ready to go."

"That won't be necessary. I feel fine."

"I'm sure you do, but we'd all feel better knowing for sure. I'll have Airman Clayborn escort you. Before you go," he said, opening the top drawer of his desk and pulling out a manila envelope, "I need you to give this to your uncle. It's eyes only, which means you're not to give it to anyone but him—nor are you to open it. For any reason." He pushed the letter-sized packet toward her.

Tess reached across the desktop and picked up the envelope. The words *Top Secret Classified* were stamped in red on the front. "Is this information about why the Russians attacked us in Moscow?"

"I don't know. That's the point of it being classified eyes only. My job, like yours, is to get the envelope to your uncle. Whatever's inside is important. That's all we need to know."

"So that's it? People just got gunned down and I'm not allowed to know why?"

Tanner paused, looking as though he was deep in thought, searching for the proper words to respond. "It's getting late, Ms. Wainwright. Let's get you checked out and fed, shall we?" He stood, aiming his hand toward the door. "I'll have someone fetch you and your friends when it's time to depart."

Tess rolled her eyes and shot to her feet, marching a path to the door in a stomp. It was all she could do to hold back the thoughts roaring in her brain. She folded the classified envelope several times, until it was small enough to shove into her back pocket.

She walked a few more steps before raised voices filled the administration section, adding to the already out-of-control twinges invading Tess' stomach.

Clayborn must have noticed the same, because she came to a sudden stop.

If Tess hadn't been paying attention, she would've collided with the woman's backside.

An older man with flushed cheeks barreled toward them from a desk in the middle of the room. "Clayborn. I've been looking for you. Beckett wants to see you," the man said, his scowl so deep it looked like a permanent fixture on his face.

"Beckett?" Clayborn asked, leaning to the side and looking past the man.

Tess did the same. Everyone was buzzing and busy, as if some calamity had just taken place.

"We have movement along the perimeter. Beckett will fill you in," the man said, flicking his eyes in Tess' direction.

Clayborn nodded, setting her feet in a more even position than before. "I need to escort the survivor to the infirmary first."

The title of survivor was a stab in the gut. Tess hadn't thought of her situation in those terms. She wanted to burst into tears and scream at the same time. "I can find it myself, if you just point me in the right direction. Don't want to be any trouble."

"My orders are to take you to the infirmary," Clayborn said, her chin high in the air, making Tess wonder if her neck might snap.

"All right then, lead the way." Tess caught a glimpse of the darkness outside. "You people must work some really long hours."

"If duty calls, we are on—no matter what."

No sooner did the woman finish her comment than an escalating sound whizzed overhead, ending in an explosion that rocked the building.

"Get down!" Clayborn said, pressing Tess to the floor and covering her with her body.

A siren screamed as a sea of troops tore their way through the room and out of the half-domed structure.

Clayborn slid off Tess and stood up, holding out a hand as the ratcheting sound of bullets being injected into rifle chambers filled the room. "Come with me."

Tess latched onto her hand, allowing Clayborn to pull her to her feet.

Clayborn shouldered her toward the back of the work area, then down a hallway about fifty feet long. There were three rooms at the end, each with an entrance door with a single narrow window about shoulder height that spanned most of the width.

Clayborn guided Tess to the last of the three rooms, opened the door and shoved her inside. "Lock the door and stay low. I'll return when it's safe."

Tess turned to find the Silent Brothers wide-eyed and standing in the corner with their infamous briefcase at their feet. She locked the door, then motioned with a finger to her lips for the two men to stay quiet. She opened a thin slit in the blind and peeked out of the window in the door.

A man in an Air Force uniform marched toward Clayborn. His face was covered in what looked like blood, distorting his features.

"Who the hell are you?" Clayborn asked, aiming her handgun at his chest.

Just as Clayborn got off a shot, the man smacked her arm away, directing the bullet into a ceiling tile. The gun fell to the floor and slid out of reach as he wrapped the fingers on one hand around her neck. The other hand held a rifle aimed at her stomach. "Where Americans?" he asked, his accent unmistakable—Russian.

"Fuck you," Clayborn answered, straining to raise her voice with his hand clamped around her throat.

Tess dropped the blind and backed away. "No, no, no," she whispered.

The rifle fired.

Tess ducked, folding her arms over her head. Moscow all over again. Her stomach wrenched as a stream of blood began seeping underneath the door. She hoped it was enemy blood, but she knew in her gut that Clayborn had just lost the fight.

Tess slid the shade open just enough to see the insurgent standing with his back to her, then after taking in his surroundings, he headed toward the first room.

Clayborn—the tall, beautiful, brave woman who'd saved her—lay bent on the floor, her eyes glassy and looking to the ceiling.

Tess wanted to curl up in the corner and cry, but after what had happened at the Center in Moscow and with Dom, there was no way she was going to let another Russian bastard kill her or the guys huddled behind her. Enough was enough.

Tess tapped the conference table, then made a pushing motion with her hands, hoping the men would understand what she wanted. "To shield us," she mouthed with her lips.

The table weighed only a few pounds and the three of them were able to tip it up and set it down without a sound. She had no idea if it would stop a bullet, but she had to do something.

Tess crouched behind it, signaling for the Silent Brothers to do the same.

"Where are Stan and Carol?" she asked in a whisper.

The Silent Brothers both snuggled in next to her and shrugged.

"Damn it, speak!" she said in a breathy voice, just above a whisper.

The non-briefcase guy took a deep breath. "La-la-last we saw—" he said with a severe stutter, using a low volume as well.

The other guy put a hand on the stutterer's arm, then took over the answer. "We were split up. I guess they could be in one of the other rooms, but I really don't know."

Tess groaned, wanting to smack herself for making that poor kid talk, trying to push the words out of his malfunctioning lips. No wonder he never said anything. All she could do was nod, fearing she might push the guy's humiliation even farther if she tried to apologize.

She stood, preparing herself to make a run for it, when a hand yanked on her shirt. When she looked at the Silent Brothers, both of them shook their heads, mouthing for her not to go.

"Yes, we leave now," she answered, stepping over a pool of blood leaking in through the gap at the bottom of the door.

Tess wasn't sure she could pull this off and stay alive in the process. Then again, she'd done things she never thought she would—all in a matter of hours—each time willing herself to victory.

So there was a chance, but she'd need help. From Stan. He had more skills than her and he seemed capable. Plus, he had knowledge of the base and perhaps Turkey.

She unlocked the door and put her shoulder against it, knowing that Clayborn's body was just on the other side. After a deep breath, she pushed hard, hoping to move the Airman's body enough to execute the next phase of her plan.

Just then, the door gave way all at once, sending her stumbling outside.

The Russian insurgent whirled around in a flash, his cheeks running red as his eyes narrowed onto her. They looked like a pair of heat-seeking missiles, preparing to slam into their target.

"Looking for someone?" she asked in her most warrior-like voice, her eyes never leaving his face. Before he could react, she dove over Clayborn's body, her hand landing on Clayborn's handgun.

Tess hit the floor chest first, making her face whip forward and smack into the polished surface. Warm liquid trickled down from her nose, landing on her lip.

She ignored the pain as she wrapped her fingers around the gun and dragged it closer.

The Russian ran at her, aiming his foot at her hand, attempting to kick the gun out of her grip.

An instant later, an explosion rumbled above, making the Russian crane his neck and peer at the ceiling.

Tess followed his eyes as the lights faded, then blinked out, leaving them in pitch black as smoke began to leak into the room.

She didn't hesitate, bringing the gun to bear as she listened for movement. She held steady and fired at the memory of where the Russian last stood, not stopping her trigger finger until the gun was empty.

After the ear-splitting barrage ended, she dropped the weapon and covered her head, bracing for some form of retaliation in case she missed.

When none came, she crawled backward, running into the body of Clayborn. She felt her way past the corpse, smearing her hands with blood as she went.

There was a flicker, then a sudden flare of light as the emergency systems came to life, sending beams through a growing smoke cloud.

Tess squinted as she coughed from both the blood from her nose and the smoke, as she looked for the Russian.

The infiltrator wasn't in front of her like before with a rifle pointed at her head. He wasn't a heap on the floor, either, dead from a bullet wound. Not as far as she could see.

Tess heard what sounded like footsteps heading away in a hurry. She grabbed the handgun once again, then shot to her feet with the weapon in a firing position, even though she knew there were no more rounds. She turned toward the sound, seeing dots of blood on the floor in the same direction. She was no expert, but thought the drops were leading away from her position.

Before she could decide what to do, the door to the first office popped open and Stan stumbled out with Carol hanging onto his arm—both coughing with watery eyes. The gash above his left eye looked deep, bleeding in streaks down his face.

"Well. Hell," he said upon arrival, spitting out his wad of gum. He cleared the blood from his face, then looked at Clayborn's corpse, blinking in rapid fashion. "Looks like I missed all the action."

"Are you okay?" Tess asked, nodding toward the door Stan had just emerged from.

"Barely. That RPG damn near took us out."

"I thought we were dead," Carol said.

"Me too," Tess added.

Stan pointed to her nose. "You do know you're bleeding, right?"

Tess sniffed, not bothering to wipe her face. She turned her head to the side and spat out the blood that had run into her mouth. "I don't have time to bleed."

Stan smiled, looking almost proud of her before he turned his attention to the trail of red drops on the floor.

"I think I hit him," Tess said.

"Nice work, kiddo. Wasn't sure you had it in you."

"Neither was I," Tess said, holding the gun out, wanting him to take it.

Stan took the weapon and ejected the magazine. "Looks like we're black on ammo," he said, tossing it to the floor.

Carol grunted as she tugged at the bottom of her cotton blouse until she tore off a long strip. She walked up to Tess and held it out to her. "For your nose, dear."

CHAPTER 9

Tess winced as she shoved the fabric that Carol gave her up her left nostril, letting it dangle from her nose.

"Nice look, Wainwright," Stan said, his tone snarky. "That'll keep the Russians at bay, for sure."

She rolled her eyes at him, then stuck her head into the meeting room where she had been hiding with the Silent Brothers. "You guys coming?"

Two dark-haired heads rose from behind the conference table that remained tipped on its side.

Carol leaned in behind her and said, "Boys!" before pushing past Tess and hugging each one.

"Come on. No time for that," Stan said.

Tess didn't say a word but she agreed with Stan. There was no time for a reunion. She had no idea what was going on outside of the building or who was left alive, never mind where they should go—she'd have to trust that Stan would take charge and keep them safe.

Stan ran his thumb over his mustache, smoothing it down over his lip. He eyed the Silent Brothers, then the briefcase, looking as though he was unsure what to do.

Tess didn't want to wait. "Colonel Tanner said he was arranging a transport plane for us."

"Assuming there was time before all hell broke loose," Carol said.

"But we have to assume, right?" Tess replied. "Otherwise what else are we going to do?"

Carol paused for a beat. "Unless everyone is already dead and we're all alone."

"Won't matter," Stan said. "Just need fuel and clear runway."

Tess grabbed his shirt. "What about a pilot?"

"Got it covered, " Stan said, pulling himself free.

Tess looked at him, holding for a beat. "You?"

He waved a hand at the group. "Follow me. I know a back way to the hangar."

Before they made it ten yards, Tess heard the distinctive ratcheting sound of a bullet being injected into a chamber.

"Halt," a man said, his Russian accent thick.

Tess stopped her feet and turned toward the hallway, seeing a man standing with a rifle at the ready.

She backed away as Stan came forward with his hands out wide, blocking the line of sight from Tess to the Russian. "Easy now, buddy."

Tess' heart skipped a beat when the Russian soldier moved to his right, bringing the rifle to bear on her. He planted his feet in a wide stance as if he were steadying himself.

She held up her arms. "Don't shoot, please."

The Russian shook the muzzle of the weapon to the side several times, his eyes focused in a long stare at a point behind her.

She swung her head around and noticed one of the Silent Brothers standing only a few inches away, holding the briefcase against his chest.

"Move," the Russian said.

Tess took a step to the side, her knee bumping into a chair sitting in front of a computer station. She scanned the Russian's body, her eyes stopping on the left side of his ribcage—the side soaked with blood and spreading fast. "Looks like I got you good."

"Not now, Tess," Stan said, taking his eyes from the soldier and furrowing his brow at her.

"Someone's gotta do something," she said, steeling herself for what she planned to do next.

"I am doing something."

"Not from where I'm standing."

"Trust me, I've got it under control."

"No talk. Quiet," the soldier said, his eyes moving from Stan to the man holding the satchel from the Embassy. "Bring me briefcase."

"Here's your briefcase, asshole," Tess snapped, picking up the chair next to her and flinging it at the soldier.

"Get down," Stan yelled.

Tess ducked for cover as the explosive sound of gunfire stabbed her ears. First it was two shots, then one immediately after, before a barrage ripped through the air, sending chunks of ceiling tiles above her into a scatter.

She crawled on all fours, tucking herself behind the control station in a ball.

One of the Silent Brothers was crouched next to her, but he wasn't the one with the briefcase.

Tess went to say something to him, but stopped when a jolt hit the desk, finding its way into her shoulder pressing against it.

A second later, a weight landed on her from above, smashing into the back of her neck and rolling forward across her head and onto the floor in a thud.

She shook off the pain, figuring a body had just landed on her. When she opened her eyes, she expected to see Stan or Carol lying there, but that's not what her eyes reported.

The body belonged to the Russian soldier, his neck bent at an awkward angle with his legs lying spread-eagle in an angled twist. There was a gaping hole in his chest, blood spilling out of the wound.

"We need to run," the man next to her said.

"Hang on," Tess said, rising up a few inches to peek around the side of the console.

She saw Stan and Carol, both standing ten feet away with wide eyes and numb looks on their faces.

Briefcase man was with them, he too apparently trying to make sense of what had just happened.

Stan brought his eyes to Tess, giving her an expression that said the threat was over.

119

Tess waved at the man hiding with her. "It's okay. Come on." She stood, brushing the ceiling tile dust off her clothes.

"Is everyone all right?" Colonel Tanner asked, stepping into view with a pistol in his hand. Two Airmen waited behind him, their rifles aimed in opposing directions, as if they were keeping watch on the rest of the area.

"Impeccable timing, Colonel," Stan said.

"Where's Clayborn?"

"She didn't make it," Stan replied.

"She was really brave, Colonel. Protected all of us," Tess said, her heart wanting to speak up for fallen hero.

Tanner held for a moment, his face running dry of concern. "The plane is ready. Time to head out."

"Colonel, what's going on here? Why did the Russians attack?" Stan asked.

"I'm sorry, but that's classified."

Stan bit his lip, looking as though his head was about to explode. "With all due respect, sir, we already know the damn Russians are here. It's not a secret anymore."

The Colonel stared at Stan in silence, his eyes pinched and blinking.

"We have a right to know after all we've been through," Tess said in a firm tone.

"As I said, it's classified."

The guards behind him each took a step to the side, acting as if their movements were scripted in some fashion.

Tanner continued. "You need to go. Now. The plane is fueled and standing by."

Stan narrowed his eyes as he balled a piece of gum between his fingers and tossed it into his mouth.

"These Airmen will escort you," Tanner said, then leaned toward Tess. "I'll make sure to get word to your uncle."

"I appreciate that, Colonel."

"Move out," the Colonel said to the guards, motioning to them for action.

One of the Airmen took the lead while the other waited for the group to pass before stepping behind Tess.

She turned around every minute or so to make sure the trailing guard was still there, giving him a smile each time. The last thing she wanted to do was smile during a crisis, but this man, like the one leading the way, was putting his life on the line for them; that was the least she could do.

His expression, on the other hand, was flat-out serious, staring at the hallway ahead with hawk-like eyes—except for the times he turned to check the area behind him.

Two more right turns and a left took them to the back of the command building, all the while Tess' heart pounded at her chest. She expected to see piles of bodies littering the corridors, with blood everywhere. They had to step over and around a few corpses, but not as many as she anticipated.

There were, however, smashed office doors and broken glass in almost every section, indicating several skirmishes had taken place. Tess couldn't believe the sheer amount of bullet holes riddling the place. It was a wonder the walls remained standing.

After they took what she figured was their last turn, a thin veil of smoke surrounded them, bringing a cough to her lungs.

"Maybe we should find another way?" Tess asked, struggling for another breath as the shooting outside grew louder.

"We have it covered, Miss," the Airman behind her answered, his hand on her back, guiding her forward.

The Airman's statement didn't sound convincing, sending the queasiness in her stomach into orbit.

Stan's posture stiffened as Carol walked closer to the Silent Brothers, giving Tess the impression her friends weren't comforted by the Airman's words, either.

Just then, the smoke lessened as the lead Airman came upon a closed door blocking their path. He held up a fist for everyone to stop.

After the Airman opened the door, he was joined by four other troops, each armed and wearing combat gear.

"Let's go, people. On the double," one of the new men said.

The Silent Brothers hesitated until Stan elbowed them out the door.

Carol looked back at Tess with her eyes wide, then ran after Stan.

Tess nodded to the Airman guarding the door and stepped outside.

The first thing she noticed was a vehicle on fire. There wasn't much left of it, but she thought it might have been a truck. Hard to tell with all the flames and smoke pouring into the air.

What struck her most was the odor. Mostly burnt plastic and rubber, all mixed together with what she thought was the smell of diesel fuel.

They continued marching along, now with two uniformed men leading the group and four others covering their rear and sides, scanning with their rifles held high—just as Tess had seen the Marines do for the escape of the Embassy crew in Moscow.

The area was alive with gunfire, bodies, and chaos, yet they worked as one unit, scoping the area, putting themselves in harm's way like the brave heroes they all were, and doing so for complete strangers, all in the name of the flag and freedom.

"Move, move, move!" the man closest to her said, his words fighting for relevance amongst the deafening pops and cracks pounding at their ears.

There was a flash of movement to her right. Tess stumbled backward as the man who had once been shoulder to shoulder with her fell to the ground. His mouth spilled open, expelling what she thought was a scream, but she couldn't hear it above the insanity around her. Fresh streaks of red ran wild around his torso and leg.

Tess squeezed her eyes shut, not wanting to see another drop of American blood.

"Tess! Move!" Stan yelled into her ear.

Her eyes flew open in an instant as she threw her arms up to cover the top of her head. The heat of the flames soaring around them felt as though it might melt her skin, making her tuck her elbows in close to her face.

Stan grabbed Carol and pushed her next to one of the uniformed men as they drew closer to what looked like an old pickup truck that had punched through a barrier and exploded.

Just beyond it was a wide metal ramp leading up to the back of a military plane.

A swarm of uniformed men stood watch, guarding the massive aircraft with their rifles buzzing with fire.

"Only a few more steps," Tess mumbled to herself, keeping her sights on the platform ahead. She coughed as the clouds of smoke thickened.

The group made it to the ramp and scampered up, arriving in only seconds.

"Where's Carol?" Stan asked once they were all inside and the engines on the plane came to life.

The Silent Brothers spun around, one of them speaking for the other. "She wa-wa-was right beside us."

Stan spun and sprinted back to where they had entered the plane.

Tess followed, staying only one step behind. She gasped as Carol's limp body was pulled up the ramp by an Airman latched onto her arms.

Stan scampered down the ramp to help, taking one of her arms from the man who'd been dragging her.

Tess couldn't take her eyes from the ring of blood growing on Carol's chest—a chest that didn't seem to be processing air.

Once the ramp raised and latched shut, the noise level dropped, allowing Tess to better hear the sound of the engines and the occasional plink of gunfire hitting metal.

Stan knelt next to Carol, picking up her hand. "It's my fault. I was supposed to protect her. She's dead because of me."

Tess put a firm hand on his shoulder, squeezing it tight as the plane began to roll forward. "It's not your fault. All of this is Russia's fault."

The troops pulled Tess and her friends to their seats on one side of the plane, helping everyone strap in for the flight.

CHAPTER 10

Ben threw his cell phone onto the passenger seat after hanging up with his latest dog-training client. He thought about punching the dash of his Jeep, but held his temper in check.

The client had a habit of rescheduling at the last minute, no matter how many confirmation messages Ben left for him. This time was no different, almost as if the man had some overwhelming desire to establish dominance through his flakiness.

Ben wished he'd reenlisted in the Army instead of giving this new business venture with civilians a go. Then he could've continued to train dogs for the military, instead of dealing with erratic clients who wanted their animals to do party tricks and other mundane chores, like fetching a beer from the fridge.

"Now we'll have to spend another night in that hellhole of a motel," Ben said to Wilma, who puffed out one of those playful, whimpering dog sighs.

He pulled onto the Las Vegas strip and took his time as he drove past the Caesar's Palace Ferris Wheel. He planned to make his next visit to Sin City more about pleasure than work, including a nighttime ride on the massive High Roller Ferris Wheel. He figured it would cost him his entire dog-training fee, but it'd be worth it. Anything to take his mind off the people he had to deal with on a daily basis. Especially in this town where anything goes.

When Ben arrived about halfway down the Strip, the traffic slowed, then stopped altogether, bringing him in behind a muddy Land Rover with one of those snorkels rising up from the side of its hood. The lime-green machine was peppered in mud and political bumper stickers—the kind that touted the end of the world was coming because of grid failures and giant solar flares.

The sidewalks on either side of the street were jammed with tourists buzzing about, some of them stopping to take pictures, while others carried drinks or shopping bags.

There were also a few women wearing skimpy outfits and looking to be avoiding a throng of police officers headed their way. Some of the cops were on foot and others were approaching on bicycles.

Two bright-red tour busses sat at opposing angles a few car lengths ahead and three lanes over.

It looked as though both of them had tried to deny the laws of physics by attempting to occupy the same space at the same time after a sudden lane change. Crumpled metal was the result. So was rising steam from their radiators as a bevy of passengers snaked their way out of the bus on the left and into the street.

Wilma must have noticed the activity, her eyes glued to the same thing he was watching.

A man in a SUV to his right opened the driver's door and stood on its side-runner, peering over the automobiles in front of him. That was about the time the chorus of horns swelled up, sounding like the brass section of a symphony warming up before a concert.

Ben rolled his eyes. "We need to get out of here," he mumbled, stabbing a glare at his rearview mirror. Perhaps there was a way to make a U-turn and escape this mess.

Before he could decide, an explosion rocked the street, sending Ben slamming into the door as a brilliant flare lit up his vision and an ear-piercing boom pounded at his eardrums.

Ben righted himself and then unhooked the seatbelt, seeing flames billowing into the sky ahead. His first instinct was to push the dog to the floorboard and join her there, so that's what he did. He closed his eyes as screams filled the air, unable to convince his body to move.

A half a minute ticked by before he managed to wrestle control from his panic and climb back into the seat behind the wheel.

The traffic jam around him was now a firestorm of panic and mayhem. What had been a straight line of vehicles was now a jumbled mess of metal on metal, the explosion tossing cars into the air and on top of one another. Bile rose in his throat as he watched victims fall to the ground, consumed in flames. The ones that were still alive crawled toward the sidewalk.

"Oh my God," he said in a whisper, his trembling hand covering his mouth.

Ben scanned the chaos, his eyes landing on the first tour bus. It was no longer a towering beacon of Las Vegas fun. The entire vehicle was on fire, turning itself into a blackened, charred skeleton, its front end bent into a mangle, as if twisted by a monstrous hand.

The explosion must've caused the companion bus to topple on its side. It lay partway onto the sidewalk with flames pouring out from the engine compartment and spreading toward its observation windows in the back.

Ben snapped the leash on Wilma, then sprang from the Jeep, leaving the door open as he pulled the Shepherd behind him. He managed to make it about ten steps before the voice of a girl brought him to a halt.

"Help me, mister. Help me," she said, sounding young. Maybe a child.

His eyes darted from one vehicle to the next, looking to pick her out amongst the wreckage and the people racing in every direction.

He walked a few more steps to the left, bumping into a man who was in the process of dragging a red-haired woman from a crumpled Subaru, its cabin starting to fill with smoke.

132

"Hey. I need your help," the man snapped at Ben, nodding in the direction of two kids in the backseat.

"I'll get them," Ben said, letting go of Wilma's leash and trying to open the passenger door with several full body yanks. It wouldn't budge, no matter how much force he was able to muster. The steel on its frame had been bent inward in two spots, leaving him few options without a hydraulic spreader or some other device.

He decided to use the driver's door instead, climbing in and leaning up and over the front seat to reach out for the kid closest to him—a little boy, maybe six years old. "Come on, give me your hand."

The child didn't move, his eyes wide and full of tears.

"Come on. Please. We have to go. I'm not going to hurt you."

Again, the boy defied his help.

Ben couldn't wait any longer as the smoke continued to thicken. He coughed, lunging over the seat and snatching the kid's arm, pulling him forward until he could lift the youngster over the seat. The boy looked to be holding his breath as he struggled against Ben's grip.

Moments after Ben delivered the boy to the pavement and put him down on his feet, he started coughing and then took off running for his mother's arms, a good twenty yards away.

Wilma barked and pranced on all fours as Ben went back into the car and hurled his torso over the seat to latch onto the little girl.

He hauled her out, taking less time to free her since he didn't bother trying to convince her to come with him first. She too, took off a second after he put her feet on the asphalt, making a beeline for her mother.

"Thanks, man," the guy said as Ben grabbed Wilma's leash.

"Glad to help."

The woman corralled both of the kids as they ran in a direction opposite of the tour busses.

"Help! Someone help me!" the same little girl's voice from before rang out.

"Where *is* she?" Ben said before whirling around. His sights landed on a body that hung halfway out of a window of an upside-down Corvette, her tiny frame wedged between the side of the coupe and the front bumper of a Ford truck.

Ben dropped Wilma's leash and sprinted toward the dangling figure.

"I'm here. I'm here. Don't move," Ben said to her, struggling to keep his voice calm.

"Help me, please. Don't leave me," the girl said through a round of sobs, tears pouring across her freckled cheeks.

He looked at the bloody hand she held in front of him, waving for him to grab it. Two fingers were shredded and hanging in clumps on the opposite of her thumb, but the girl may not have been aware.

Ben slipped his favorite Seattle Seahawks long sleeve shirt over his head and took it in his hands, folding it in thirds. He wrapped it around her mangled digits and managed to tie it off around her wrist using the material from his sleeves.

"Please mister. Hurry," she said, her face white and arms flailing for him to do something.

"I will, I promise," Ben said, tucking his hands under her waist, trying to leverage her free, but she wouldn't budge. "Can you lift up a little for me?"

She nodded, her face contorting as she made the attempt to wriggle up and off the window frame. "I can't. I'm stuck."

"What's stuck?"

"I think it's my shirt."

"Okay, hang on," he said, noticing the flames to his right had jumped to a set of cars two lanes over from their position. His face was hit with the smell of burnt rubber and the heat of burning fuel, bringing a new wave of adrenaline to his body.

Ben moved his hand to the right side of her waist, feeling around the fabric. His hand came in contact with a piece of metal that was long, thin, and bent in the middle, making him think it was a hunk of aluminum from the window frame. He traced its length, finding that it continued on, entering the fabric of her shirt at an angle.

He repositioned his fingers, wrapping their tips around the material where it met the metal. He dug his nails in and yanked until the cloth ripped free from the jagged end. "Okay, try now."

Her torso lifted just enough for him to slip his arm all the way around her. "Okay, I'm going to try to pull you out."

She didn't respond as he leaned back and began to pull her out, hoping she wouldn't get caught on anything else.

When her legs cleared the window, he squeezed her to his chest and ran across the street, taking a path through the maze of cars.

He put her down on the sidewalk just as a female officer arrived and knelt down next to the girl.

"I'll take it from here," the woman told him, wrapping a blanket around the girl before picking her up and taking her toward an L-shaped building on the corner.

Just before the entrance door closed behind them, the girl turned her eyes toward Ben and gave him a smile and a quick wave with her mangled hand still wrapped in his shirt.

He sent a grin back and gave her a thumbs up signal.

After a pair of hands landed on Ben's shirtless back, a man's deep-toned voice said, "You okay, buddy?"

Ben turned to the voice, seeing a heavyset man with a handlebar mustache. "I'm fine."

Just then, Wilma arrived and pushed in between them, plopping her hind end on one of Ben's shoes.

"I take it she's yours?" the man asked.

Ben nodded but didn't respond, rubbing her collar with two hands.

"I think the cops are setting up a triage center down the block."

"I'm fine, but thanks," Ben said as the man took off to the right, weaving his way through the scene.

A wail of sirens screamed in the distance, their howl growing louder with each passing second. Ben knew it wouldn't be long before the area would be locked down by law enforcement and emergency crews. He needed to get his suitcase from the Jeep, grab a shirt, and get out of here before everyone else headed for the nearest cab stand.

Before he could take a step, Wilma took off in a sprint, heading straight into the fray to his right.

"Wilma, come back here," he called out, but she kept running. He took off after her, dodging cars and people along the way, trying to keep his eyes on her.

When he caught up to her a minute later, he saw Wilma dragging a woman by one of her pant legs, her body limp as if she were a ragdoll.

"Great job, girl," Ben told her, keeping his hands from touching her fur, not wanting not to interrupt the dog's mission—a hard rule he had instituted for his military-trained dogs.

Ben bent down and propped the woman's head, neck, and torso on his legs. He could see her chest processing air, the rise and fall of her pink tube top evident.

Wilma continued to yank and pull on the woman's pants as Ben lugged her by her underarms across the street and over to the triage station.

"What do we have here?" one of the medical crew asked him when he arrived in the lobby of the building. The man's height bordered on freakish—he was huge, pressing the scale at something around three hundred pounds if Ben had to guess. All of it muscle with a waistline smaller than his.

"Not sure," Ben replied, gasping for air. "My dog found her and brought her to me."

"Your dog?"

"Yes, she's trained for this."

"How long has the victim been unconscious?"

"The whole time, though I could see she was still breathing. Didn't know what else to do but bring her here. I hope I didn't screw something up?"

"We'll take it from here," the medic said, ignoring Ben's question and beginning his triage of the victim.

Ben took a few steps back and knelt down on one knee, letting a long sigh escape. Wilma snuggled in next to him. He gave her a tight squeeze, then got to his feet and took her by the leash, moving toward the middle of the room.

The lobby was crammed with wounded and emergency personnel. The shiny marble tile was covered with streaks of blood and gauze, the smell of smoke growing more intense the farther he waded into the throng.

He stopped one of the uniformed personnel with a clutch of his hand. "Excuse me, officer, is there anything else I can do to help?"

"Thanks for the offer," the officer said, his tone deep and gravelly, as if he had a load of pebbles in his mouth, "but I think it's best if you—"

The man's response was cut short when a thunderous blast ricocheted off the walls, sending the cop hurling to the floor on his side.

Ben felt the impact slam into his chest, toppling him backwards in a thud. An instant later, something smacked the side of his head, bringing a wave of dizziness and pain with it.

He lay there for a few seconds, trying to bring his senses back online as screams bit at his ears. He felt Wilma press up against him, her fur tingling the hairs on his arm. She whined, then brought the wetness of her nose to the skin on his cheek.

After the rumble stopped, Ben heard someone say, "Hey, are you all right?" He recognized the tone. It was the same gravelly voice of the cop.

"I think so," Ben said, sitting upright. His head throbbed as he touched the impact site on the side of his head. There was a lump forming, but his fingers came away clean. "How about you?"

The man never answered, instead pushing off the floor and pointing out of the building.

Ben brought his eyes around and saw a brown UPS delivery truck on fire, only a few yards from the blown-out windows that used to line the lobby.

Ben followed the man's lead and stood, keeping watch on the truck fire and the mass of smoke it sent into the sky. His view became blocked when a series of fireman arrived, aiming their hoses at the blaze.

Just then, he realized that if the UPS truck explosion had gone off thirty seconds earlier, he, Wilma, and the tube top woman would've been at ground zero. The thought sent a pressure wave across his chest, taking a good portion of his breath away. However, the feeling vanished a second later when he felt the buzz of his cell phone in his pocket.

He took out the device and looked at the screen. There were three new texts waiting. One of them was from his dad and it was stamped with a time from fifteen minutes earlier.

Tess at private airbase. I'll send coordinates shortly. Get her ASAP. Don't stop for anything. No matter what. I've cleared you for entry. Ask for Ambassador Hudson. He's there. Hurry!

CHAPTER 11

"What the hell?" Ben Wainwright said from behind the wheel of his Jeep when he saw the flames shooting into the sky ahead.

He clamped his eyes shut for a moment, then opened them again, taking another look to confirm what his eyes were reporting.

The fire was indeed coming from somewhere on the private Nevada airbase—not far beyond the wooden shack guarding the front gate.

He checked the GPS unit again, confirming the coordinates matched what his father had sent him.

"This has to be it, girl. Nothing else out here for miles," he told Wilma. The knot in his stomach doubled as he drove closer, adding to the anxiety already coursing through his veins from the anarchy on the Las Vegas Strip earlier that day.

Wilma must have sensed something was wrong, too, picking her head off the seat and then sitting up with her ears pointing straight up.

"Tess will be okay," Ben told the dog, giving her a quick rub with an outstretched hand. He added pressure to the gas pedal, closing the distance to the guard shack at twice the previous speed.

There weren't any signs indicating the name of the base, but there was plenty of activity in sight. Transport trucks, fuel trucks, and cargo planes sat on a flight line he could see off in the distance, plus there were huge storage tanks sitting above ground to his right.

He wasn't surprised when he saw Humvees scurrying about inside the fenced-off area that was topped by razor wire. But he didn't expect to see men in street clothes, wearing combat vests just like those in military uniforms and boots.

Ben slammed on the brakes a minute later, just short of the gate, sending his Jeep into a slight skid.

The guard standing in front of the shack looked to be young. Almost too young for duty such as this—barely eighteen or nineteen, if Ben had to guess.

The young man was outfitted in a full camo uniform, with a sidearm strapped to his thigh. The gun inside the holster would be easily accessible in a quick draw if something went sideways.

The helmet across his head looked to be a size too big and the name stenciled on his shirt was Ruger.

Other than the name badge, there were no American flags or other designations on the sleeve. Just a chest rig with extra mags and what he assumed was body armor underneath.

Ben recognized the military spec rifle in the guard's hands. It was an M4 carbine, hanging on a sling from high to low across his chest. He'd shot one of those in his days of service and remembered the weapon well. It was an air-cooled, direct impingement, gas-operated, magazine-fed hunter/killer. He preferred to keep his in its three-round burst firing mode, while others on his fire team always chose semi-auto, each man using their own preferred setting.

The guard drew his head away, flashing his eyes in the same direction as the smoke filling the air, then brought them back to Ben, with his hands clutching his rifle.

"I'm sorry, the base is closed," Ruger said, his voice clipped, almost as if he were disinterested in Ben's arrival.

"I'm Benjamin Wainwright, Senator Wainwright's son. I'm supposed to have clearance," he replied, sticking his hand into his pocket. He dug around for his wallet, pulling it free a second later.

When he went to yank out his driver's license, he fumbled the wallet, sending money and credit cards sprawling to the floor.

He bent down to scoop up the pile just as Ruger said, "We're on lockdown until the base commander gives us the all clear."

Ben pointed ahead. "Please call Ambassador Hudson. He's supposed to be inside. He's expecting me."

Ruger held firm, his jaw stiff and lips silent.

Ben wasn't willing to accept no as an answer. Not unless he planned to face the wrath of his father, who was explicit with the words in his text: *Don't stop for anything. No matter what. Hurry.*

He swallowed a sticky lump of saliva, forcing the bulge down his throat. It felt as though someone had dumped a truckload of cotton into his mouth, then tossed in a vat of glue for good measure. "I'm here to escort one of your VIPs. Her name is Tess. As in Tess Wainwright."

"Sister?" the guard asked.

"No, cousin. That's why my dad, Senator Wainwright, sent me. To pick her up."

"Senator Wainwright? Never heard of him."

"Well, he's real and he gave me explicit orders to pick her up and not to stop for anything. It's urgent."

The man shook his head, looking more defiant than before. "My orders are clear."

"So are mine," Ben said, gripping the steering wheel even harder with his fingers. "Look, despite what you don't know, my father is a very powerful Senator in Washington and will have my ass. Yours, too, if you don't let me in. So please, do both of us a huge favor and let me in. Or call the Ambassador. Either way works."

The guard only blinked, keeping his mouth clamped shut.

Ben continued, feeling the need to drive home his point. "Trust me. My old man is not the kind of man you want to disappoint. He's the Chairman of the

Senate Armed Forces Committee. I'm sure you've heard of them, right? They're on the news like every other day, talking about the vote coming up on the new military budget."

The tips of Ruger's fingers released from the rifle, then clamped down again, his boots shifting in place as he stood. That's when the man's eyes pinched, then swung to the left, scanning the inside of the base.

Ben could feel the thickness in the air triple, making his lungs pump air even faster. He let his eyes drift from the man, landing in a long stare aimed across the hood of his Jeep.

He needed a moment to calculate the consequences for his failure. The kind of failure that might get him disowned, after stopping to help strangers on the Las Vegas Strip after the explosions rocked the area, instead of getting his ass here to pick up Tess as ordered. He'd never forgive himself if something happened to her. Neither would his dad.

Ben brought his attention back to the guard. "Hey, I get it. You have a job to do. So do I. But this is urgent. As in urgent Washington business. Just call your boss and ask for Ambassador Hudson. He'll explain it all. He's supposed to be waiting inside for me."

"Turn around now. This is your last warning," Ruger said in a sharper tone than before. A second later, he brought the barrel of his weapon around and aimed it at Ben.

Every cell in Ben's body screamed at him to slam the gear shift into reverse and get the hell out of there. Yet for some reason he couldn't convince his hands to move.

Something else was in control of his body. He wasn't sure what it was, but it wasn't his logic, that's for sure. "Yeah, right. Nice try, dude. Like you're really going to shoot the son of a sitting Senator. A world famous one at that."

Ben thought about telling the guard about the incident at his father's house with a couple of no-neck guys that may have had something to do with everything going on, but decided against it when a call came over the base's communication system, taking the guard's attention away.

"Hold here," Ruger said, flashing a level hand before spinning and walking inside the shack.

Ben let the Jeep crawl forward until he was even with the door of the shack, giving him a better view inside. He wondered if the ambassador had just called and scolded the young man for not allowing entry.

A split second after Ruger spun his shoulders and bent down to write something on the desk in front of him, an explosion rocked the base.

The compression wave slammed into the Jeep, making Ben duck out of instinct. When he brought his head back up, he could see another towering set of flames, twisting a billow of smoke into the air.

Ben decided he couldn't wait any longer, snapping his fingers to tell Wilma to get down. The German Shepherd did as he commanded, sliding off the seat and lying on the floor in a curl of legs and fur.

After a deep gulp of air, Ben slid his foot off the brake and slammed it against the accelerator.

The vehicle shot forward, smashing its chromed-out grille into the swing arm protecting the gate. The barrier blew apart, sending wood and metal into the air, as the Jeep made its way inside.

Ben turned his head to glance back, wondering if Ruger was now outside and drawing down on his position. He could see the shack and the broken pieces of the gate arm, but there was no sign of the kid with the rifle.

The road split off in two directions about three hundred yards ahead. One of the branches headed left, toward both sets of flames raging in the sky.

The other would take him to the right, between two buildings that looked like warehouses. Or hangars. He couldn't be sure with all the smoke, but they were huge, stretching on for what seemed like forever.

Ben turned the wheel, choosing the second option, leaning forward and never letting his foot off the accelerator. He'd hoped the smoke would lessen as he went, but it didn't, making him wonder if he'd ever find Tess.

That's when he saw them—two military-style Jeeps with their emergency lights flashing—heading his way as they tore around the far end of the hangars.

Right behind them was what appeared to be a Humvee loaded with men standing on the running boards, like some kind of SWAT team rolling out.

Shit. They were going to arrest him for breaching security. He was screwed, soon to be incarcerated and a branded a complete failure in the eyes of his father.

Ben slowed, trying to come up with an escape plan. Yet his mind only fluttered, consumed with random thoughts of metal bars and handcuffs, then hours of scolding and finger pointing from his old man.

The area on either side of him was blocked by the buildings. His only choices were to reverse course or play a game of chicken with armed men on a mission to detain him.

He stomped on the brakes and turned the wheel, bringing the Jeep to a quick halt along the side of the road. Before he could decide what to do, he noticed the convoy wasn't slowing. In fact, it appeared that they had picked up speed. Maybe they weren't coming for him after all?

Ben decided to slump down in his seat as they cruised past him, keeping his eyes just above the bottom of the window.

That's when he spotted the BSF insignia on their left armbands, just below a yellow and black flag he didn't recognize.

It had a strange circular design in the center, like a logo. Red in color. He figured the BSF initials on their sleeves meant Base Security Force.

"Must be their version of MPs," he mumbled, wondering if this installation was some kind of secret CIA rendition site, far away from anything remotely civilian. Or military, for that matter.

Next up, a fire truck raced into view, following the same path as the security patrol, its siren blaring as it rolled past him in a rumble of mass and intensity.

Ben waited until the convoy and fire truck were well behind him, then brought the Jeep back onto the pavement to resume his hunt for Tess.

When he cleared the rear of the buildings, he slowed to dodge a wave of troops scrambling on foot. They seemed to be everywhere—both male and female—heading in multiple directions at once, all of them wearing stunned looks.

At least nobody seemed to be paying much attention to him, allowing him to travel unaccosted, albeit at a pace far slower than he needed.

Ben decided to angle left, toward a squadron of cars and trucks sitting unattended, each one positioned within the white lines of a parking lot.

Dozens of vehicles meant dozens of people. Hopefully, administrative types. As in maybe Tess was inside, waiting for him, with the ambassador at her side.

He chose a parking space between two black cars. Both SUVs. Good to blend in.

"All right, girl. Let's go find her," he said to his loyal passenger. "I wish I had something with her scent on it. You'd find her in a heartbeat, and we'd be outta here."

CHAPTER 12

Ben clipped a leash to Wilma's walking harness and they headed toward the dome-shaped building ahead. As soon as they reached the front of the building, three women exited, one right after another, all of them in a fast walk, looking intense.

A tall brunette zipped by him first, speaking in a harsh tone on a cell phone. "Yes, significant damage. Might be more, we just don't know."

The other two women, both with blonde hair, bent together and conversed in a whisper as they closed in on his position.

Ben leaned down, pretending to fix Wilma's collar to keep his face hidden, just in case they'd been alerted about his breach.

The moment after they walked past, he rushed forward and grabbed the handle of the door and opened it, letting Wilma slip in first.

They cruised through a central foyer with potted plants and a few motivational posters along the walls.

Up next was a spacious area filled with desks and people. Some were in the same all-camo uniforms, matching what Ruger wore at the front gate. Others had street clothes on, some in three-piece suits, each with a charged look on their face.

The sheer volume of voices stabbed at his ears. So did the incessant ringing of phones, making it hard for him to think.

Whatever had just rocked the base had sent everyone into action, with their arms waving and papers moving from desk to desk.

Ben angled to the right, figuring it was smart to walk the perimeter. Less conspicuous, especially with a group of uniformed men standing in a knot near the center of the room.

A few civilians hovered with them, everyone with their eyes glued on a gray-haired gentleman in the middle. His pressed suit and red tie screamed man in charge.

The buzz of adrenaline in the room was the perfect cover, he decided, giving him time to move unnoticed as his mind ran through different scenarios about what he would offer for answers if he were stopped and questioned.

Sure, he was the son of a distinguished Senator, but that status wouldn't help much if he ran into a trigger-happy guard who preferred to shoot first and ask questions later.

If this was a secret CIA base, then there was no telling what their rules of engagement would be, especially out here in the middle of the Nevada desert, far away from anything official.

Ben shortened the leash on Wilma and lowered his head, keeping their pace smooth and consistent, not wanting to draw attention.

No sooner did they make it to the end of the adjacent wall than a man's voice rang out in their direction. "Hey, you—the guy with the dog—"

Ben did a double-take when a round-shaped man in a wrinkled business suit huffed and puffed his way toward him.

The guy's stride was a mix of locked knees, heavy shoulder sways, and arm pumps, his four hundred pounds of carb-eating indulgence affecting his speed.

By the time the red-faced guy made it to Ben, there were streams of sweat pouring from his temples, almost as if he'd spent all day in the sun and then took a shower. "Where's your ID badge?"

Before Ben could respond, the man's face puckered, almost swallowing itself. His skin turned a strange purple color for a few beats, then it went all-white a moment later.

"You all right?" Ben asked.

The guy opened his mouth to answer but the only thing that escaped his lips was a grimace-filled gasp. Then he grabbed his chest and doubled over, crashing into the floor in an awkward twist, landing on his side.

"Medic! Help! I need a medic over here!" Ben yelled over the chaos without thinking.

He dropped Wilma's leash and held out a firm hand. "Stay, girl."

Wilma complied as Ben kneeled next to the man and used both hands to roll the behemoth over and onto his back.

He then brought his fingers together and began chest compressions, fighting through his own jitters to remember his CPR training. He was supposed to give the man mouth-to-mouth, too, but couldn't convince himself to do it, not with the oozing drool leaking from the guy's mouth.

In truth, he never should have stopped to help a stranger. Not just because of the mouth-to-mouth issues, either. More so because, after his incident at the front gate, a smarter man would have ignored the apparent heart attack victim and kept on walking.

The last thing an insurgent does is stop to help anyone when armed guards are on the hunt for him.

Ben didn't how long he'd been working the man's sternum before two medics arrived, but he was glad they did. He'd done all he could—well, mostly. Plus, his arms were tired and the man was still unresponsive.

He shifted his weight back and rolled to his feet, watching the medics take over the resuscitation protocol. He picked up Wilma's leash and scanned the layout, needing to get moving.

Luck and distractions had gotten him this far, but he figured neither would continue. This might be his last opportunity to work his way deeper into the building.

He skirted around the medics and three onlookers who'd just arrived, using quick steps to finish his trek through what he assumed was the remainder of the administrative department.

"Got any ideas?" he asked Wilma after they sailed through a rear door and into a hallway that branched off in three directions.

Wilma bounced from side to side, looking up at Ben.

"Come on, girl. Give me something. Otherwise, I'm just guessing here."

Wilma pranced for a few seconds, then shot to the left, pulling at Ben's arm in a lurch. He stumbled to regain his balance as the dog led him forward in a trot.

When the canine looked back at him, he said, "Yeah, I feel it too. Keep going, girl. We'll find her."

They made it around a corner and to the right without running into anyone.

Above him was a sign that said *INFIRMARY*. Next to it was another one that had been stenciled with the word *CHAPEL*. A third said *MESS HALL*.

Each placard pointed in the same direction—straight ahead, down a sparse hallway that had been painted a dull shade of gray.

Ben let Wilma continue her hunt, her nose sniffing at the floor in a sweeping pattern.

She stopped to check a few objects along the way, the first being a wooden hallway bench. Then it was a stainless-steel water fountain, before a vending machine filled with nothing but bottled water grabbed her attention.

Ben caught up to her and yanked her forward. "Come on. That's not Tess," he told the dog, unable to stop thinking about the connection of the infirmary to the explosions outside. "Let's just hope she's not hurt."

His gut was telling him to turn around and avoid the infirmary. There would be far too many people inside, especially right now.

Yet his heart screamed at him to continue, so that's what he did.

Tess was here somewhere and she needed him. He could feel it in his bones.

Wilma ran ahead, resuming the search with her snout close to the floor.

There were four doors ahead, two on either side. None of them looked to be labeled. Not with words, anyway. Only numbers with hyphens between the numerals.

He figured they were storage rooms or possibly empty offices. No way to know for sure. Hopefully they were not sleeping quarters or something else filled with trained personnel. The kind who would know he didn't belong.

Ben stopped to yank the first door open, figuring he'd never get that lucky and find Tess right away, but he had to try nonetheless.

The room, like the one next to it, was used for storage, just as he assumed. Linens and medical supplies were in stacks that filled the entire space, almost as if someone had done so to stop anyone from entering.

What caught his eye next were the four boxes, each about the size of a microwave oven. They had the same red insignia he saw in the middle of the yellow flag earlier. Plus, their shipping labels had a return address somewhere in Seattle, with a company name listed: *International Science and Technology Laboratories Inc.*

"What are they preparing for? The apocalypse?" he said to himself. Then again, this was the CIA presumably, stocking more stuff than they could ever use.

He continued, checking the third door. The room was the same size as the others, only this one was filled with electronic equipment. Old parts and broken gear were the dominant items, all of them covered in dust.

The last room was mostly empty. Only a mop, a rolling yellow bucket, and an empty jug of bleach with its cap missing. There was an Arizona Highways calendar hanging from a nail on the wall. Its month and year said April 1995.

"Damn, that's been there a while," he quipped to himself.

Ben closed the door with a soft click just as the sound of boots came stomping across the floor, growing louder. It was coming from behind him.

He whirled around and met the eyes of an armed man who had turned the corner at the far end only moments before.

The man's eyes were sharp and his hands were latched onto a rifle hanging at an angle across his chest. Ben assumed it was another M4, like the guard at the front gate carried.

"Hold it right there," the man called out, sounding like one of the unflappable MPs from his days in the service.

Wilma barked at the guy, then Ben turned and ran with her in the opposite direction, taking a connecting hallway to the right.

It was another all-gray corridor that opened up about twenty strides later into what he assumed was the triage zone for the infirmary.

His feet drove him straight into the herd of doctors and nurses tending to the wounded. Everywhere he looked, he saw bodies with burns and plenty of blood.

He worked his way through the wave of casualties, trying to avoid bumping into anyone or making eye contact.

Wilma seemed to know what to do, leading the way like a hound dog navigating the hunt.

A handful of steps later, a masked female doctor with long blonde hair and narrow shoulders stood up and turned, bringing her face around to Ben.

"Are you all right, sir? Do you need medical assistance?"

She was one of the prettiest women he'd ever seen, with blue eyes and smooth skin. It took Ben a moment to gather himself before answering. "No, no. I'm good. Thanks."

The physician glanced down at Wilma, narrowing her eyes in the process.

Ben wasn't sure what she was thinking, but it probably wasn't good.

For a moment, he thought about covering his ass and telling her Wilma was a search dog brought in to help with the incidents. But he couldn't fib to that beautiful face. Besides, he sucked at lying and the explosions had just occurred. There wouldn't have been time to call for any help yet.

Wilma leaned up against his leg, which snapped him back to reality.

The doctor relaxed her expression and gave him a quick nod, ridding Ben of the tightness in his chest. Since she didn't seem to be eyeing him like a criminal, he decided a quick question might help his search.

"Actually, maybe you can help me. I'm looking for Tess Wainwright. About your height, dark hair. Do you know if she's here? I can't seem to find her anywhere."

The woman shook her head and shrugged. "Sorry. Try the nurse's station. They're logging in all the wounded."

Ben couldn't help but smile at her, but that ended when he heard the distinctive sound of boots hitting the floor. He didn't have to turn around to verify who'd just arrived. He knew from the deep voice he heard next. "Coming through. Make a hole."

Ben's face dropped as the doc's grin faded. She peered around Ben and held for a beat, then flicked her eyes to his.

"Nurse's station?" Ben asked, pointing to the chest-high counter along the wall to his right.

She turned to peer at the location he'd indicated, then gave him a firm nod.

A quick survey of the area told Ben that the MP would be there in only a few strides. However, if the roles were reversed and he was the cop, the nurse's station would be the first place he would check.

Ben decided he'd have to blend in and wait it out until the time was right to slip past the man and resume his search for Tess. He leaned forward to lessen his profile, then ducked to the left, weaving deeper into a thicket of wounded.

There were limbs missing on several victims who weren't burned, not something he'd expect from the ignition of jet fuel.

That told him the explosions must have been something more powerful. Something intentional, perhaps, planned with malice. It would better explain the scramble to lock down the base and the scurry of activity.

He paused for a moment and scanned the area once again. If Tess was here, he couldn't see her, but there were sections ahead with curtains hanging on tracks in a horseshoe pattern. He assumed beds were inside. Probably filled with the most severely injured.

Ben moved ahead, glancing inside each medical bay to see who it contained.

The first was empty, but there was blood on the floor and a container filled with red gauze and other medical waste. Whoever was in there wasn't any more.

The second, third, and fourth bays were busy with nurses attending to victims. Most of them were men and all of them were burned.

There was one with a female; however, her hair was stark gray, and her weight must have clocked in at double that of Tess.

Ben continued his trek, selecting a path to the last sectioned-off area, stopping at the edge of the hanging fabric. He knelt down and pretended to tie his shoe as he peered inside.

A female nurse was attending to a bandaged man whose head was on a pillow, with his eyes closed. His burns appeared to cover his entire body, plus his left arm was missing.

"Damn," he whispered to the dog as she nestled in next to him.

Drool dripped from the victim's mouth, leaking from the corners in what Ben could only describe as a bubbling gurgle.

Ben assumed it was from the painkillers the nurse was probably giving him with the IV bag dangling on a pole next to the bed.

Right then, the woman inside spun on her heels and walked to a countertop on the right, bringing her face around in Ben's direction.

Ben leaned back, using the edge of the curtain to conceal his face. If she decided to leave her patient and walk outside, he was screwed.

He took a moment to look back at the nurse's station, checking for the cop. Sure enough, the guy with the BSF armband was standing there, just as Ben predicted, with his back to Ben's position.

Before he could decide where to go next, the hot doctor—the woman of his dreams—pointed at the first bed with a curtain surrounding it. The cop swung his head around and stared in the direction she pointed.

Ben ducked lower, angling his body behind a couple of people standing about ten feet from his position, attending to a skinny girl lying on her side. He needed a way out. Someplace other than the door he came in, but he couldn't just stand up and look. The cop would see him. Or the pretty physician would and rat him out—again.

He'd have to stay low and guess, hoping the triage area had a back door somewhere. He looked at Wilma. "Got any ideas? Now would be the time."

Wilma brought her eyes around and looked up, just as someone cleared their throat behind Ben.

Ben whirled around and craned his neck up to see who it was.

"Hey, you can't be in here with that damn dog," a young male nurse said. He stared at Ben with his nose scrunched, then tipped his head to the side as if to say, *Why are you still here?*

"Sorry, right. I was just leaving anyway," Ben replied, shortening Wilma's leash before he stood up, keeping the man between him and the cop.

The guy pointed to his right. "Front door's over there."

"Is there a shorter way? My dog really needs to drop a deuce. Would hate for her to do that here. You know, germs and all."

The man paused for a beat, then pointed to the left this time. "Fire exit. Just past Recovery. Go."

Ben turned and made a beeline in the direction the man had pointed. He thought about looking back to see if anyone was following him, but decided against it. Either the cop was onto him or he wasn't. Looking back wouldn't help, only slowing him down and drawing extra attention.

CHAPTER 13

When Ben passed the overhead sign that said Recovery, a new idea slammed into his mind.

"Let's go in here," he said to Wilma, yanking on her leash to turn.

They went through the doorway, entering yet another hall. This one was lined with at least a dozen doors, all closed.

Each entrance had a clear acrylic holder attached to the wall next to it. The opening for each holder was at the top and angled away from the wall. Most of them appeared to contain clipboards, but a couple looked to be empty.

"Charts," he said to Wilma, before stopping next to the first door. He didn't see anybody, so he reached up and grabbed the clipboard from the holder in front of him.

The name on the paperwork attached to it said *Jerry C*. There was also a bunch of mumbo-jumbo written on it in physician speak. Something about pistons or pistols. He couldn't be sure. The handwriting was a mess.

Ben slid it back into its spot and continued down the corridor, checking each medical chart he came across. There were names like *Dennis R*, *Rocket H*, *Dave L*, *Don N* and one *John Doe*, but not a single female listed.

"Shit. Where is she?" Ben said, stopping in front of the second-to-last door. This one didn't have a chart in its holder.

That's when he heard it: a conversation beyond the door. He leaned in with his ear. The discussion inside was a bit muffled, but he could hear three different voices: two men and a woman.

Wilma brought her nose to the bottom of the door and began sniffing the air leaking out from the circulation inside.

"Is she in there, girl?"

Wilma sat down and brought her head up.

"You've got something, don't you?"

173

Ben put his hand out to grab the doorknob, but the door swung open on its own and he found himself standing eye-to-eye with a burly, gray-haired man dressed in a blue pinstriped suit and matching tie. The guy even had a white handkerchief that had been folded and tucked into the front pocket of the suit coat.

"Whoa. Sorry. Didn't expect anyone to be standing there," Ben said.

The man looked down at Wilma, then back at Ben. "I take it you're Mr. Wainwright. I'm Ambassador Hudson. Been waiting for you."

Ben couldn't believe it. Somehow luck had brought him here. And in one piece. "Ah, yeah. Got held up at gate. Literally."

"They were supposed to escort you in. I left specific instructions."

"Sorry, Ambassador. I tried to tell the guard, but the dude didn't seem to care."

"I'm sure the lockdown had something to do with it. Even I can't overrule a base commander in a time of emergency," Hudson said, turning sideways and inviting Ben in with an outstretched hand.

"Really, even on a CIA base?" Ben asked, hoping to answer a few questions burning a hole in his mind.

"Not CIA," Hudson replied.

Ben stepped forward with Wilma, seeing a woman lying on her side in a bed with a blanket pulled up to her nose.

There was also a tall guy with shaggy black hair standing next to her, wearing a white lab coat and holding a clipboard with paperwork on it. The top page was curled up in his hand, giving him access to whatever was written on page two.

The patient's hair hung down across her eyes, so Ben couldn't see her face. He increased his speed to a fast walk. "Tess?"

The man in the lab coat stopped Ben with an arm bar. His ID badge said Dr. Rogers. "I'm sorry, but that's not your friend."

Ben looked back at Hudson, then at Rogers, trying to reconcile the situation in his head. None of it made sense. "Then who the hell is it?"

Just then, the door to the room's private bathroom swung open and out walked Tess with a grin on her face. "Ben, you made it!"

"Barely," he said as Wilma shot forward and jumped, landing her front paws on Tess. "Are you okay?"

Tess nodded, then hugged and rubbed the animal. "Hi, girl. I've missed you."

Tess let go of Wilma and sat in a chair next to the hospital bed. She bent down and tied the laces of her sneakers, as if nothing odd was happening.

Ben pointed to the bed. "Who's that?"

"A girl we found outside the Mess Hall."

"Tess and I were headed here for her quick checkup when we ran across her," Hudson said.

Ben threw up his hands. "Where is here, exactly?"

"What do you mean?"

"I mean, who's footing the bill? Because this place is frickin' huge—I know it's not the Air Force."

"I'm sorry, but I'm not at liberty to say."

Ben figured the Washington suit would say those exact words. Maybe if he guessed correctly, it would free the man up to reveal the truth. A portion of it anyway. "Some kind of secret black site? For renditions, maybe?"

"I already told you, this is not CIA."

176

"Then who is it? I saw that yellow flag."

"Some friends of ours. Patriots, to be sure. All you need to know is that we're all on the same team."

Ben shrugged, realizing Hudson was just like his dad—always talking in cryptic riddles, answering questions in a nondescript way. He figured they must teach all members of Washington this specific skill when they first arrived. Some kind of mandatory spin class, he decided. Something called Obfuscating 101. It was all about uttering plenty of words but never really saying anything.

Ben looked at the girl on the bed. "What's wrong with her?"

"Still trying to assess," the doctor answered, his hand busy scribbling something on her chart.

Ben turned to Hudson. "So it's got nothing to do with what's going on outside?"

"Not a thing, as far as we know."

Ben pointed at the door. "Then what is all that out there? Something's going on, because shit doesn't just blow up like that. Not twice."

"Just a little trouble with a disgruntled employee, I'm afraid. But they're getting it under control."

"Employee? As in corporate?"

"Yes, someone decided that sabotaging two fuel depots would make a statement."

"Ya think? It's chaos out there."

"Apparently, that same someone wanted to get themselves fired. With prejudice."

"I'd say he accomplished his goal," Ben said, wondering if Hudson would at least admit the perpetrator was a man.

Hudson didn't bite, his lips remaining pressed together.

"At least we had some advance warning," Dr. Rogers said, still fumbling with the paperwork.

"Not that the injured would agree," Hudson replied.

Tess walked to Ben, wrapping him a strong, two-armed hug.

Ben reciprocated, realizing that Tess and her hug were the only two things that made any sense. Oh, and Wilma, too.

"I've missed you," she said into his shirt.

"Same here."

After Ben let go of Tess, the door to the room swung open with a swoosh and in walked the policeman who was in hot pursuit from before. The guy pointed at Ben. "Hold it right there."

Hudson stepped in front of the guard, whose nametag on his shirt pocket said Keel. "Son, you need to stand down."

"That man is under arrest."

"No, he's not," Hudson said, pulling out something from inside the lapel of his suit coat. It was a black bifold. He turned it sideways before opening it and aiming it at Keel. "I'm Ambassador Hudson." He shot an emphatic nod at Ben. "That man is Ben Wainwright and he has full clearance."

"No sir, he breached the front gate. We have it on video."

"That's all well and good, but I left specific instructions for your team to allow him entry. He was supposed to be escorted here as soon as he arrived."

"We were on lockdown, sir."

"And that matters to me how? My orders are clear and so were yours. Senator Wainwright—this man's father—was the one who arranged the pass. The Senator is the Chairman of the Senate Armed Forces Committee in Washington."

"That's what I tried to tell that Ruger guy at the front gate," Ben said, throwing up his arms in disgust. "But the asshole just pointed his M4 at me. I thought for sure he was going to shoot, so I took off when he turned his back for a second to take a call. That's when the second explosion went off."

Keel didn't respond, the tension in his face lessening a bit.

Hudson continued, "For your sake, Keel, and the sake of your career, I'd suggest that you check in with your C.O. I'm sure he'll explain it to you."

The cop stood his ground, bringing his eyes to the doctor, apparently looking for guidance.

"It's okay, Brian. I'll take it from here," Rogers said.

"Are you sure, Doc?"

"Yes. Absolutely."

"As you wish, but I'm going to take a position outside," Keel said. "In case you need me."

"That's fine," Rogers answered.

The group waited in silence as the cop left the room. Once the door closed, Hudson stepped closer to Ben and Tess, then put a hand on each of their shoulders.

180

Ben leaned toward him.

So did Tess.

Hudson looked over his shoulder, glancing at the door for a moment, before bringing his eyes back to Ben. "The Senator was explicit. Once you were reunited with Tess, we are to get you out of here and on your way home. ASAP."

"Which home? We have several."

"Seattle."

"Okay, the cabin," Ben said, thinking about the retreat he'd spent his summers at during his youth.

"The one in the woods?" Tess asked.

Ben nodded. "Yep. The place we used to ride my dirt bike all around."

Ben's mind switched channels again, showing him a visual of the boxes he ran across in one of the storage rooms. Specifically, the four containers with the shipping labels from an address somewhere in Seattle.

His gut was telling him that it was all connected somehow, but he wasn't going to raise the question with Hudson. The man wouldn't answer him anyway. Plus, he didn't want to tip his hand that he knew anything about the name of the company printed on them, either.

It was better to keep quiet and wait until they made it to the cabin, then he could figure out some of this craziness on his own. That was the only way to get some real answers, he figured. Answers he could trust. "Are we flying? Because I've got my Jeep outside. Don't really want to leave it here. Not with all the bullshit going on."

"No, he wants you to drive. Take the back roads. Keep your heads down."

"Back roads? That's insane. It'll take forever. The freeways are faster," Ben said.

"I'm just the messenger, son."

"Are we in danger?" Tess asked with a pinched face.

"Everyone is, young lady. Don't trust anyone. Can't stress that enough."

"What the hell is going on?" Ben asked, thinking about the altercation with the men at his father's house earlier and the subsequent pandemonium on the Las Vegas Strip. "Because everywhere I go, it seems like society is coming apart at the seams. Never seen anything like it."

"You know I can't tell you anything more. My job is to get you on your way. So please, just do as your father asks. I'm sure he'll explain it once you get her to the cabin."

"Is he meeting us there?"

Hudson paused for a moment, as if he was contemplating relaying the truth for once. "I'll walk you out. Did you park out front or somewhere else?"

Ben sighed, scolding himself in silence for even asking. "Front, I think. But I've never been here before, so who knows?"

"Were there a lot of cars?"

"Yep, most of the spaces were filled."

"Follow me," Hudson said, leading Ben, Tess, and Wilma through a maze of hallways. He opened a door at the end of the fifth corridor, allowing a beam of brilliant sunlight to shoot inside.

Hudson squinted and pointed to the left. "The parking lot is that way."

"What about security?" Ben asked. "I'm sure my face is on their top ten most wanted list right about now."

"I'll cover it with the Base Commander. You need to get moving."

183

"Thanks Ambassador," Tess said, leaning in and giving him a peck on the cheek. "For everything."

Hudson gave her a weak smile. "I'll get a message to the Senator. Now hurry."

Ben wrapped Wilma's leash tighter in his palm, then used his other hand to grab Tess. Despite what Hudson had said, he still felt compelled to look left then right to make sure the area was clear of cops.

"Let's go," he said before the three of them took off, jogging around the side of the building, not stopping until they reached the Jeep. He yanked both passenger doors open and pointed inside the rear door. "Wilma, down."

The dog hopped in and lay on the back seat in a curl.

Ben shut the door with a gentle hand, then sprinted around to the driver's side, noticing that the smell of smoke was much more prevalent than before. And the sky was blacker than he remembered on his way in.

Tess got in and planted her butt in the passenger seat, then closed the door with a soft touch, just as he had done for Wilma.

Ben climbed in and scooted himself behind the wheel, running through a list of questions in his mind. There were so many, he wasn't sure where to start. He fired the engine and stomped on the gas, deciding to wait with the Q and A. He needed to keep sharp until they were clear, and that meant no conversation.

When they drove over the splintered pieces of the front gate and zipped past the guard booth, Ben swung his head and looked inside. The shack was empty. So was the surrounding area. No sign of Ruger or his pals.

It didn't make sense, but neither did anything else today.

CHAPTER 14

"Hey, aren't we supposed to take back roads?" Tess asked, seeing the Interstate sign zip past her window.

"The freeway is faster. If we see anything weird, we'll hop off."

"Well, now you jinxed it," Tess said, flipping the visor down in front of her and opening the cover on the mirror. She sucked in a breath when she saw her face.

She should have known better. No one on their best day should ever check themselves in a car mirror, and especially not after running for their life in Russia, having no clean clothes, and being dehydrated. And needing a shower. She snapped it closed. "I look like crap."

"Yeah, I was going to say something about that," Ben said after a chuckle.

"Shut. Up."

"No really, do you want to stop at a store to get some clothes or something? Wouldn't take long. It's not like anybody would know."

"Nah, not after what Ambassador Hudson said. We should just head to the cabin."

Ben leaned toward her and sniffed the air. "Are you sure? Getting kind of ripe in here."

She punched his shoulder. "Knock it off."

Tess wanted to joke around with Ben like they used to do, when they'd laugh until their stomach muscles cramped, but that was long before everything that happened the day before in Moscow and Turkey.

"Can you believe all of Hudson's bullshit back there?" Ben asked.

"What do you mean?"

"A disgruntled employee. Seriously?"

"I guess it's possible. But I think it was someone else."

"Who?"

Tess could've smacked herself. She knew she'd have to talk about what happened in Russia at some point. She just wasn't up for the recount or a debate. Not with Ben. Not with anyone. Her eyelids felt like someone had parked a cement truck on them. All she wanted was sleep. And a bath.

Plus, she didn't want Ben to worry. Not after her heart rate had just returned to normal. The last thing she needed was any more excitement. Or stress.

She turned her eyes to the window, letting her gaze run into a long stare, not focusing on anything in particular passing by.

"Hey, you all right over there?" Ben asked after thirty seconds of silence.

"Sorry," Tess said, seeing what looked like an old camper shell sitting on top of a cactus. "So what do you think really happened?"

"I don't know, but I'd put my money on someone who doesn't like International Science and Technology Laboratories Inc."

Tess whipped her head around to Ben. "Why would you say that name?"

"Because it was all over these boxes I found in a supply room when I was looking for you."

Tess couldn't believe she'd heard that company name again. And so soon. "Seems obvious to me. They probably own the airbase."

"Why would you think that?"

188

She thought about holding the answer back but was too tired to argue with herself. "Because that was the name on the helicopter that got us out of Moscow."

"Yeah, right," he said with a smirk on his face. "Now you're just yanking my chain."

"No, I'm serious. It's all got to be related."

Ben didn't reply right away, his eyes peering at her for a beat. "Yeah, maybe. But Moscow? What the hell happened over there?"

She sucked in another quick breath and held it for a few seconds, then let it escape in a slow puff of air. It was clear he wanted information and she couldn't blame him, but she wasn't ready. "I'll tell you everything, I promise—just not right now."

He laughed. "Did I tell you that after I snuck into the building to rescue you, this huge guy had a heart attack? Right there in front of me, while I was talking to him. I shit you not."

"Rescue me? Yeah, right. That cop was ready to haul you away. If it weren't for the Ambassador, then—"

"I'm not kidding. Collapsed right at my feet. I had to do CPR on him."

189

"Well, at least you saved somebody today."

"Thanks. I love you, too, cuz."

She shook her head as Wilma came forward in the back seat, pressing her nose into Tess' cheek. Tess rubbed her friend's neck. "I'm just glad we're out of there in one piece. This has been one messed-up couple of days."

Tess let go of Wilma and returned her attention to the landscape cruising past the window outside. There were large round shrubs that grew in random patches along the side of the freeway. She pointed, then looked at Ben. "Hey, don't those turn into tumbleweeds when they die?"

"Okay, I get it. Changing the subject," Ben said. He shifted his butt in the seat before moving his line of sight from the rearview mirror to the side mirror and back again several times.

"Is something wrong?" Tess asked.

"That car behind us—"

Tess whirled around to see a car a few hundred yards behind them. It was in the same lane and looked to be matching their speed. "You mean that white sedan with all the chrome?"

190

"Been there a while now," Ben said. "Time to get off the freeway." He jammed on the accelerator, swerving to the right as they hit the exit ramp, heading down the pavement at a sharp angle.

Tess grabbed the dash in front of her and pressed her feet into the floorboard, locking her knees in the process. "Hey, easy does it."

"I think that's the same car from before."

"What are you talking about?"

"Right before I headed to Vegas, I stopped to see my dad and saw a car just like that one. It was parked out front when I got there. Then these two mafia-type guys came running out the front door after they literally gave my dad a beatdown."

"A beatdown? Is he okay?"

"He said it was nothing—which was a load of crap, just like everything else that's happened recently."

"And you just left him there? You should have called an ambulance."

"Come on, you know him as well as I do. Once the great Senator makes up his mind and tells you something, you accept it. End of story. He said it was nothing and told me to leave. Wasn't much else I could do."

"You still could have called 9-1-1 after you left."

"Yeah, that would have gone over well—not," he replied, working the steering wheel. "When my dad tells you to do something, you do it. Otherwise, you never hear the end of it. Ever."

"I suppose."

Ben veered onto a one-lane road, bouncing over several potholes. The marker read *Badwater Basin.*

"Geez," Tess said, feeling every dip and bump in her back.

"Yeah, no lie. Reminds me of D.C."

"They should've named this road Pothole Alley. They could swallow us whole," Tess said as they followed a sharp curve in the road.

That's when she spotted it—a shiny object looming ahead of them.

She squinted to better assess the item.

It appeared to be a twisted piece of metal and it wasn't moving. She pointed at it. "Ben, watch out."

"I see it." He swerved to the right, clipping the edge of the object.

That's when she realized it was a royal blue bumper but it didn't clink like metal. Must have been plastic or fiberglass, she decided.

"Where did that come from?" Ben asked.

The answer came a hundred feet later, when they saw an overturned car just off the dirt on the shoulder opposite from them, its trunk facing the roadway.

The vehicle was royal blue, just like the bumper, and it was small. Shoebox small, like something you'd see driving around Europe—barely a two-seater. Its hood sat on top of a green bush with yellow flowers poking out from the sides.

Ben slowed the Jeep and veered to the side of the road before slamming on the brakes, sending the tires into a full skid. Dust plumed upward, covering the area in a blanket of orange muck.

Once the air cleared, Tess saw the top half of a woman's body sticking out from under the upside-down car. She could see the model name on the back of the car. It said BOLT with the letters EV after it.

There was an older man with her in the dirt. He was on his knees, with his gray beard reaching down to his legs, ZZ Top style. Plus he had on blue coveralls and suspenders.

A tall, muscular man with slicked-back hair and a bright white bandage on the side of his neck stood next to the old man, his face chiseled and his jaw stiff.

CHAPTER 15

Tess hopped out of the Jeep and ran to the edge where the dirt met the pavement. She looked both ways, then ran across the road. Ben and Wilma followed a few steps behind her.

Tess made it to the towering guy with the bandage, puffing hard after the sprint.

When he spun to make eye contact with her, she realized he had another bandage on the other side of his neck. Both of them were the size of a deck of playing cards, as if he'd just had the worst shaving accident ever.

"What can I do to help?" Tess asked the hulk, noticing his arms were covered in a blanket of tattoos.

"Her husband's already called 9-1-1," he said, nodding at the gray-haired man.

Ben arrived a moment later with Wilma on a leash. "What are you waiting for? We need to get her out of there."

"Working on it," the bandaged man said.

Tess looked at Ben, then down at the woman, whose eyes were open. "They've already called for help."

Ben shook his head. "But how long is that going to take way out here?"

Tess shrugged, looking up at the man with tattoos.

"He's right," the bandaged man said. "It might be a while."

"Maybe if we worked together," Tess said. "We could—"

"No, please. Leave her be," the old man said. "Like I already told Jack, help will be here soon."

Ben touched the old man on the shoulder. "But what if it's not? Do you really want to take that chance? She might bleed to death."

The old man didn't answer.

Tess bent down and looked through the car window. She could see what looked like a raised indent about three feet long and heading away from her, pressing up and into the top of the vehicle's cab.

It looked to be about where she thought the old woman's legs should be, matching the same angle, length, and location of what she envisioned.

Ben looked at the guy with the neck wounds. "Like Tess said, maybe if we work together?"

Tess nodded, aiming her gaze at the brute the old man had just called Jack. "If Ben and I helped you, we might be able to rock it up far enough to pull her free."

"Or maybe just use a jack," Ben said, looking at the old man. "You have one, right?"

"No, it's a rental," the guy said. "Just our luggage in the trunk."

"Are you sure? Because I think they still have them. I should check," Ben said, taking a step.

Jack grabbed his arm. "I don't think that's a good idea."

"Why?"

"Don't want to take the chance it might shift the weight."

The old man nodded. "All our luggage would fall out. No telling how the balance would change."

"What about your Jeep?" Jack asked.

Ben shrugged. "Took the jack out to make room for my new speakers."

"Really?" Tess asked, not believing what she just heard.

"Yeah, I have Triple-A, so I figured what the hell."

"Damn it," Tess snapped. She was about to say more, but Jack held up his hand, stopping her lips from delivering the next thing on her mind.

Jack sounded certain when he said, "Don't think it would've helped anyway. Not in this dirt. Too unstable."

The old man nodded. "Plus we'd have to lift the car first to get the jack under there."

"What about the hood?" Tess said, pointing at the bush being squashed. "Maybe the jack could reach it."

"Nah, it's too far up," Jack said.

"Then there's no choice. We've got to lift it, somehow," Tess said.

Jack didn't answer right away, his eyes indicating he was thinking about the idea. A few seconds later, he said, "Worth a try. Probably only need a few inches."

Tess put her hands on the vehicle. "Like I said, if we can rock it a bit, maybe..."

"No. No. No. Please," the old man said, holding his wife's hand, rubbing the skin with his thumb.

"It'll be okay, Harold," the old woman said, her voice calmer than Tess expected. She must have been in pain with the car on her legs, but her face didn't indicate she was feeling anything. It was possible the dirt was helping to soften the pressure underneath. Or she was in shock.

"I'm worried about you, that's all," Harold said. "I can't lose you."

"Let them try, honey. Please. I'm starting to lose the feeling in my legs. I don't think that's good."

Harold's face turned white before he spoke. "No, Delores. It's too dangerous."

"Please, Harold. I don't want to be here anymore. I just want to go home."

"I know, honey. Me too."

"Then please, let them try. I'm begging you."

Ben looked at Jack. "She said to try?"

Jack looked at Tess and raised an eyebrow. Then he gave her a shoulder lean and a face pinch.

Tess understood the gesture. She bent down and nudged Harold, causing him to let go of his wife's hand and stand up. "We're going to get her out. But you'll need to be strong and help."

"How?"

"Pull her free when I tell you," Jack said to Harold.

The old man nodded, though it wasn't a convincing nod.

Wilma eased forward and sniffed Delores' hair, then circled around in a tight spin before folding her paws under her body and lying next to the victim.

"Dog can't stay there," Jack said.

Ben snapped his fingers. "Come here, girl."

Wilma shot to her feet and trotted to Ben. He pointed to a spot behind him. "Go there, sit." The Shepherd followed his commands.

Tess stepped forward. "Okay, where do we grab on?"

Jack lowered his eyes and held them on the coupe. A few moments later, he grabbed the bottom of his t-shirt and pulled it off. He held it out. "Cover her face with this."

Jo Nash, Jay J. Falconer, M.L. Banner

Tess took the man's top, but couldn't help staring at all his tattoos. They were everywhere across his chest and back. Some depicted animals. Others had heavy numbers above them. There were even a few disturbing symbols. Symbols she recognized. Symbols that made her stomach clench and her heart beat even faster.

"Hey," Jack said to her, shaking the garment in front of her eyes. "Take this."

"What? Oh, I'm sorry," Tess said, snapping out of her trance. "Why?"

"Gonna break the window."

Tess nodded. "So we can grab on."

"Good idea," Ben said, taking Jack's shirt from Tess and putting it over the victim's face. He leaned in close to Delores. "Go ahead and close your eyes. We're going break the glass. This will keep it off you."

"How are you going to break it?" Tess asked Jack.

He held a foot out. "Steel-toed boot."

"Okay, cool."

Jack brought his leg back and kicked at the window. The glass shattered on the first try, sending shards sprawling across the pavement.

"Now what?" Tess said, seeing a ring of jagged glass still clinging to the window frame.

"Shit," Jack said.

Ben peeled his shirt off, just like Jack had done. "Here, use mine."

Jack didn't hesitate, taking the shirt and rolling it up into a wad before using it to knock the rest of the shards free from the frame. He gave the garment back to Ben.

Ben unrolled it and shook it out like a dirty rug, freeing a few pieces of glass. He tucked it over his head and put it back on.

Jack grabbed the edge of the window frame, then peered at Tess. "On three—ready?"

Tess stepped forward and so did Ben, cramming in next to each other. Ben wrapped his hands under the edge first, then Tess did the same.

"Okay, 1-2-3, lift," Jack said.

All three grunted and yanked up.

Tess could feel the burn in her legs, but a second later, the coupe began to rock a bit.

"You okay, Delores?" Harold asked.

"Yes, yes, yes. Keep going."

"Almost there," Jack said through his clenched teeth. "Get ready, Harold."

Harold bent down and latched onto his wife's elbows, tears streaming down his face.

"Now," Jack told him.

Harold leaned back and pulled.

Delores slid out a foot.

Wilma barked, now prancing in the dirt to their left.

"Again," Jack said.

Harold tugged once more, his face covered in a full-on grimace.

Delores slid out another foot, maybe more, dragging a mound of dirt with her.

"Can you move your legs?" Jack asked her.

"I'll try," Delores said. She let out a moan, then swung her legs out, freeing them from under the vehicle.

Tess kept her knees locked and hands in place as she looked down, wondering if the woman's legs were mangled. There was no sign of blood. She couldn't believe it.

"Okay, let's put it down," Jack said. "Ready?"

"Go for it," Ben said, his teeth pressed together.

"Now."

The three of them let the vehicle drop, backing away in a collective step.

Jack stood with his hands on his hips sucking in quick, deep breaths. "She all right?"

Tess wondered the same thing, kneeling down next to Delores. "How are your legs, dear? Can you move your toes?"

"Yeah, but they're a little numb."

Ben huffed an exaggerated breath. "Looks like you got really lucky, ma'am. The dirt must have cradled your legs."

"Thank God," Harold said, hugging his wife, who was now sitting up.

Delores reached beyond Harold's back and grabbed Tess' hand. She squeezed. "Thank you."

Tess couldn't help but smile, feeling damn proud. "Just doing what anyone else would do."

"I'm not so sure about that," Jack said.

"Well, *you* did."

Ben cleared his throat. "With a little help from us."

Delores turned her eyes to Jack and then to Ben. "Bless you. I can't thank you enough. All of you."

Before Tess could respond, sirens came blaring into her ears. She looked down the road to see two State Trooper squad cars and an ambulance, all with their lights flashing. A tow truck was right behind them, tearing across the pavement.

"Looks like the cavalry is here," Ben said, looking at Harold.

Harold didn't answer, his arms still wrapped around Delores.

"You kids don't need to stick around, if you have somewhere to be," Jack said. "I'll take it from here."

"Actually, we do have somewhere to be," Ben said, tugging on Tess' arm.

"Are you sure?" Tess asked Jack.

The man nodded. "I've got this."

Tess and Ben said their goodbyes to Harold and Delores as the first responders parked and ran onto the scene.

Ben wrapped Wilma's leash in the palm of his hand and the three of them ran across the street to the Jeep.

"I can't believe anyone survived that," Tess said, after climbing into the passenger seat. She closed the door.

"Especially in that tin can. God, those things are small."

"Still, I can't believe Jack lifted it."

"Well, like I said before, he *did* have some help," Ben said, starting the engine.

"Barely. I'm pretty sure he was doing all of the work."

"I don't know about that, but I'm glad she's okay. I thought Harold was going to totally lose it there for a minute." Ben looked over his shoulder, then put the Jeep into gear and pulled out, pressing on the accelerator. He peered over at Tess. "Did you see those bandages?"

"How could I miss them? And those tattoos."

"Yeah, they were insane. I'm guessing he did some prison time or something."

"That's not all, I'm sure."

"What do you mean?"

206

"I'm thinking there's a big, long story behind all of it. Especially whatever happened to his neck."

"No doubt. He was one big dude."

"He looked like he could move a mountain all by himself."

"Or at least scare the hell out of one," Ben added, laughing.

CHAPTER 16

A few miles down the road, Tess saw a green roadway sign fly by her window. "Looks like some place called *Gabby's Grill* is at the next exit." She leaned over and examined the gauges on the dashboard.

Ben looked at her, then at the instruments in front of him. "Yeah, I know. Getting low."

"Maybe there's a gas station, too?"

"If nothing else, I need some food. I could eat the ass out of a rhinoceros right now."

"You know that's totally disgusting, right?"

"Yeah, but I'm fungry."

She laughed, unable to keep a smile from erupting. "Yeah, me too."

"Food first, then we'll figure out the fuel situation."

They made it to the exit and took it, driving a few hundred more feet before a grinding bang interrupted Tess' thoughts.

The sound reverberated across the frame of the four-by-four. It was followed by a strange, erratic flapping sound.

Tess looked over and watched Ben strain to keep control of the steering wheel.

Ben hit the brakes and turned the wheel to the right. "Seriously?"

"What?"

"Blowout," he said, bringing the Jeep to a stop. He slammed the gearshift into park and turned off the engine.

"Maybe it's not that bad?"

Ben looked at her with a crooked grin on his mug. "It's a flat. It's already bad. No jack, remember?"

"In more ways than one."

"Funny."

She shrugged, seeing a vision of the tattooed man in her thoughts. "At least it didn't involve a rhino."

Ben rolled his eyes and waved at her. "Come on. Let's take a look."

She climbed out and met up with Ben. The front tire on the driver's side had been shredded to pieces.

Ben shook his head. "Looks like we're walking from here."

Tess turned and peered down the road. There was nothing but trees and endless pavement as far as she could see. "Might be a long walk."

"Figures. This day just keeps getting better and better."

"Hey, at least we're still alive."

"Well, there's that."

"And we helped save someone today."

"Like the universe cares. All we got for our troubles was a frickin' blown tire. Can you grab Wilma?"

"Sure," Tess said, opening the back door.

Wilma hopped out and began sniffing at the ground.

Tess grabbed her leash and took a step down the road, but stopped when a new idea popped into her brain. She whirled to Ben. "Hey, wait a minute, don't you have Triple-A?"

"Ah. Well. Sort of."

"What does that mean?"

"Was low on funds and decided to wait a couple of months to renew."

"So it expired?"

"Yep."

"Well, that was a wise move."

"What's a guy to do? Needed cash to entertain the ladies."

"Yeah, right," Tess said. "I take it your dad hasn't been kicking anything in."

"Nope, I just have the money I make from dog training. And that never lasts long. He thinks he's teaching me to live within my means or whatever."

"Maybe you need to do less entertaining?"

"I was just kidding about that. But then again, when you're in demand, you're in demand."

Tess held her tongue. Joking or not, once Ben started down that path, it was best to change the channel. Or shut up all together.

They walked a few miles, passing a pair of culverts with water running through them and a slew of open fields filled with weeds.

A short distance beyond them was the first sign of civilization—a town. It looked to be about a mile ahead, at the top of a gentle rise in the road.

"Finally," Ben said. "They better have a tow truck or I'm going to go Bundy on somebody."

Before Tess could answer, an ambulance flew past in silence, without its lights flashing.

Ben looked at Tess. "You think that's her?"

"Probably."

"Why no lights? You'd think they'd be in a hurry."

"Or maybe they're not," she said in a hesitant tone.

"Good point."

"I hope something didn't happen after we left."

Ben shrugged. "She seemed okay."

Not far behind the ambulance was a flatbed truck carrying a mangled blue Chevy Bolt that had been strapped onto its back.

Tess tried to catch the driver's attention with a wave, but his eyes appeared to be burning a hole into the ambulance in front of him.

When Tess moved her eyes from the driver to the passenger, she saw the bandaged man, Jack, riding

212

shotgun. His head was leaning against the glass and his eyes were closed.

"Damn it, we should've been on the lookout," Ben said.

"No big deal. It's not that far."

They continued on foot until the edge of town met their feet. There were a few buildings, but little else.

Ben snickered. "Talk about your average shithole in the middle of nowhere."

"Well, at lease there is a shithole. You know, for those of us who don't carry spare tires or a jack."

"A to Z Body Shop," Ben said, pointing at a sign on the right, a short walk past the café. "That'll work."

"See, things are looking up."

On the other side of the road was the *Badwater Motel*. Its sign was reminiscent of something you'd see on old Route 66. The bright red logo had a yellow swoosh across the front—to Tess, it looked like a huge check mark.

The next thing Tess knew, a sudden cracking sound ripped through the air. "Get down," she screamed as she threw herself to the ground, bringing Wilma down with her.

"Whoa, easy," Ben said before squatting down next to her. "It was just backfire."

"I thought someone was shooting at us. Again."

"You mean shooting at you. Again."

"Yeah, me," Tess said, crawling to her knees.

"I get it. But you really don't need to be so jumpy. Nobody knows we're here. You're safe. Trust me." Ben pointed to a vintage forest-green Mustang sitting in front of the café, its tailpipe billowing out smoke in random bursts of black. "Just some P.O.S."

"Sorry, been a long day."

He stood, holding his hand out. "Why don't you go chill in the restaurant? I'll head over to the body shop and see what I can do about my Jeep."

She grabbed his hand and let him leverage her up, still holding Wilma's leash in her other hand. She held out the restraint to him. "Your turn."

He took it, pulling Wilma close to his legs. "Go ahead and take a load off. Have a beer or something. You're way too intense."

"Yeah, okay. Thanks," she said, running her hands over her clothes. There was dust everywhere, making her look even more of a mess than she felt at the moment.

She wished she had taken Ben up on his offer to take her shopping earlier, then maybe, just maybe, the rest of the day would have gone a lot smoother.

Tess walked to *Gabby's Grill* and went inside the swinging glass door, where a bell rang above her. The smell of fried eggs and burnt coffee assaulted her nose, bringing with it a familiar visual from her memories.

What she wouldn't give for a Starbucks latte and a fluffy croissant. Something sweet and delicious. Not some slop served by a greasy spoon trying to unload its previous week's menu. She could almost hear the arteries of the patrons around her clogging.

There were three booths with red high-backed seats lining the front wall, only a foot from the front window that spanned at least twenty feet. She looked, but there wasn't a single mark on the glass. Or a smudge. Even way out here in podunk-ville.

Unfortunately, the floor wasn't as spotless as the glass, meaning the window had someone tasked to it with a squeegee and some Windex. Probably twice a day, with all the dust flying around outside.

A horseshoe-shaped counter filled the other side of the restaurant. There was a boy, maybe six years old, wearing a Spiderman t-shirt on one of the seats.

Just then, the kid pushed off the counter with his hands, twirling himself around on the gold-flecked swivel stool. He continued to spin at least ten more times before he lost his balance and fell off. He hit the tile floor in a sideways flop, cracking his elbow by the sound of it.

That's when the boy crying started, sending a high-pitched scream of bloody murder into the air.

A woman in her thirties turned around next to him, dropping to the floor. It didn't take long for the red-haired lady to wrap her arms around the kid in a swarm of hugs and kisses. She helped him back into his seat once he stopped wailing like he'd just been shot.

Tess walked past the mother and child, choosing a stool at the far end of the counter. She plunked her butt down, then looked down at her hands. Her fingers and her palms wouldn't stop shaking, no matter what she tried.

"Damn backfire," she said in a mumble just about the time a round, two-hundred pound waitress arrived with her beehive hairdo, a menu, and a pot of coffee.

Her nametag said Sally. "What did you say, honey?"

Tess wrapped her hands together. "Nothing. Just talking to myself. Sorry."

"No worries. We get that a lot around here." The woman held the pot out. "Coffee?"

"Please," Tess answered, grabbing an empty cup that had been sitting in front of her. She held it up.

The woman filled it in a flash, then turned and walked away.

There was a widescreen television anchored to the wall above her on a tilted mount. One of the news channels was playing with the sound off.

Tess thought about asking Sally to turn up the volume, but in truth, she couldn't care less about the news. Or what they had to say.

It was always the same drivel day after day, most of it fake news anyway. Plus, it seemed unlikely that there'd be anything in the broadcast about the massacre in Moscow, or about what had happened earlier at the private airbase.

When a rush of wind blew past her, it took her attention from the TV. Someone had just walked behind her, from left to right.

She turned to see it was a man. A towering, muscular man, with bandages on his neck and tattoos covering his arms.

Jack was back.

Her heartbeat shot up a level.

He claimed the stool two spots down from her, plopping his camo-green military-style duffle bag next to it.

The waitress was on him in a flash, handing him a menu. "Can I help you, handsome?"

"Just water. Bottled," he replied, his husky voice resonating off the wall and across the room.

"It that all?" the waitress asked in a sly manner, offering him a wink.

He seemed to ignore her gesture, dropping his eyes to scan the menu, then brought his gaze back up. "Can I get a turkey sandwich to go? Hold the mayo."

"Sure, I think we can handle that. Anything else?"

The brute shook his head and gave the menu back to her.

Once the waitress finished scribbling on her notepad and walked away, Tess cleared her throat and waited for the man with slicked-back hair to look her way.

When he did, she winked like Sally had just done, but for different reasons. "Well, hi there, stranger. Long time, no see."

"Hey there, Tess."

"Delores okay?"

"Roger that," Jack said. "EMTs thought she was going to be fine. Just a concussion and some bruises."

"Wow, that's amazing."

Jack nodded. "Can't argue with you there."

"She seemed like a nice lady."

"What's the food like here?"

"Don't know. Just sat down," Tess said, sliding over a seat. "So how did their car flip over, anyway?"

"Not sure, but Harold said he hit a pothole and lost control."

"Must have been some pothole."

"Copy that."

"So you weren't in the car with them?"

He shook his head, twisting a lip along with it. "Just happened upon the crash as I was making my way down the road."

Sally buzzed in out of nowhere, holding a bottle of water. She put it down in front of Jack and winked again, then did a heel spin before heading toward a blonde, teenage girl, who had both of her arms up and was waving at Sally from the other end of the counter.

"Well, lucky for them," Tess said, taking a sip of her coffee. The instant the swill hit her lips, she spat it out. "Oh, nasty."

Jack held the bottle up and laughed. "Hence the $H2O$."

Tess smirked. "Yeah, I'm thinking that's going to be my go-to move from now on. At least when I'm out here in Mayberry-land. All we need is Barney and his friend Goober and the scene is complete."

Jack chuckled again. "Now there's a visual. Aren't you a little too young to know about that show?"

"It's called cable, Jack. You should try it."

"Who has time? I gotta keep moving."

Tess looked down at his duffle bag. "Traveling light, I see."

There was a flash on the television and both of them peered up. A news announcement streamed across the bottom of the screen in bold letters:

39 CONFIRMED DEAD AFTER CATEGORY EF-5 TORNADO LEVELS SMALL TOWN IN CENTRAL KANSAS.

"It's that time of year," Tess said in a downtrodden tone as the feed changed to show the devastation. The city was gone, leaving only a smattering of debris scattered about.

When the camera swung around, Tess saw horses and dogs running loose. So, too, were the emergency crews. "All those poor people."

"Finger of God," Jack said.

"I wonder if they had any warning?"

"Probably not. Looks like someone leveled the place with mortars."

Tess nodded, wondering if all of his obvious military lingo meant he wanted her to ask if he ever served. After a moment of reflection, she decided not to, since his eyes weren't trained on her.

She pointed at the screen instead, acting as if she hadn't noticed his obvious sayings. "If I lived there, the first thing I'd do is build the biggest damn bunker I could, and never leave."

"Bunker, huh?" he said in a curious tone. "Yeah, I like that. That's good. Bunker."

She was about to ask him what he meant, but the front door of the restaurant opened, sending the bell above it into a jingling tirade. The sound of a sputtering diesel engine wafted into the café.

Tess and Jack turned toward the door, just as Ben stuck his head inside and said across the room, "Tess, got a spare. Let's rock."

"Okay, give me a sec," she replied, fishing into her pocket for some money.

"Let me get it," Jack said, pulling out his wallet.

"No, you don't have to do that."

"Yes, I do. If you hadn't stopped—"

"Seriously, I can pay."

222

Jack slapped a twenty dollar bill on the counter, keeping his hand over it for a few seconds. "My treat."

"No, no, no. I can pay my own way."

"I said, my treat."

She could tell by the look on his face that he was annoyed by her push back. "Okay, thanks. But next time, it's on me."

"Deal."

She leaned over and kissed him on the cheek, then shot to her feet and headed for the door. After three steps, a new idea stormed her brain. She turned back to him. "Um, do you need a ride or anything? We're headed north. To Washington. The state."

"Nope," he said, pulling what looked like a paper ticket from his pocket. "Already got it covered, but thanks."

"Okay. Bye, Jack. Take care of yourself. It's crazy out there."

Once outside, she noticed two men arguing next to a gray GMC truck near the open bay of the repair shop. The entire side of the dually truck was covered in politically-charged stickers: *Epstein didn't hang himself. NASA is a hoax. FlatEarth101.com.*

"That didn't take long. For the tire, I mean," Tess said when she met up with Ben and Wilma.

"Helps when you slip the owner a little extra cashola."

Tess rolled her eyes, then nodded toward the two men by the dually truck. "So what's all that?"

He snorted and shook his head. "Weird, right? Apparently, the guy with the truck is not happy about the bill. He's been yelling at the mechanic the whole time."

A moment later, the quarrel elevated to a who-could-swear-the-loudest contest, until the disgruntled GMC owner pulled a gun.

"Ben, he has a Glock," Tess said, grabbing his arm.

"Let's go," Ben replied, pulling her in the opposite direction. All three of them ran to the Jeep, jumped in and closed the doors.

Tess kept her eyes locked on the altercation as Ben backed out of the parking space.

Then a gunshot rang out.

She ducked.

Ben pushed the accelerator to the floor, sending the tires into a screech. "Our lady of blessed acceleration, don't fail me now."

As soon as the *Gabby's Grill* sign was a speck in the mirror by Tess' window, Ben let his foot off the gas and asked, "Hey, wait a minute. How did you know that was a Glock? You don't even like guns."

Tess knew she'd screwed up. But she was going to have to answer Ben's questions at some point. Now was as good a time as any. "Ah, well. You see. I had to use one in Moscow, right after the Russians stormed my work and started killing everyone."

CHAPTER 17

"What? The Russians killed everyone?" Ben asked as his stomach churned. "You're joking, right?"

"No. I'm not joking. I'm serious. As in deadly serious."

"That's not even a little funny, Tess."

"I know. Trust me. There's nothing funny about what happened. A lot of good people died. Innocent people," Tess said, looking down at her hands as she twisted and squeezed her fingers, turning them white. "They just burst through the door of the American Center and started shooting. I was so scared, I could hardly think. It was horrible, Ben. Just horrible."

Ben paused, letting the words soak in as he struggled to keep the vehicle centered in the lane as he drove. "When Dad said you'd been through a lot, I had no idea. Why didn't you tell me?"

226

"To be honest, I didn't know how. I don't think I've even begun to wrap my head around it— never mind trying to explain it to someone else. Those were my friends, Ben. People I cared about. Gunned down like it was nothing."

"No wonder you freaked out when that Mustang backfired."

She bit her lip and nodded.

After another pause, Ben snuck a peek at his cousin to see if he should continue asking questions. Tears had begun to drip down her cheeks, but that was understandable. So he decided to fire again. He had to know more. "Why would they do that? The Russians, I mean. Just walk in and start shooting?"

"Who the hell knows? But it happened. Just like I said. One minute we were trying to figure out why the computers weren't working and the next, a truckload of soldiers had rifles pointed at our faces. Everybody ran, but they just picked off people in the back. Oh my God, all that screaming and there was blood everywhere—"

Tess ran her hands through her hair, her eyes streaming even more tears than before. Her breathing had turned choppy, too, sucking air in rapid bursts.

227

Ben knew the signs. She would shut down any minute. Still, he needed to push her, otherwise he'd never get her talk again. Ever. The problem was, he had too many questions. They were all important, but he didn't know which one to go with next.

"Something must have sparked it. Did they say anything? When you say they killed everyone, do you mean everyone? And how the hell did you get out?"

"Ben," Tess said with power in her voice, pounding on the dashboard with her fist. "I just can't deal with all this. Not now. Just get me home."

"Sorry, sorry. Just trying to process all this. It's crazy shit."

She let out an exaggerated, air-filled sigh through her lips. "Tell me about it."

"When I'm stressed out, I find it best to confide in someone else. Talking always seems to help. So I'm here, Tess, anytime you want to talk. I'll listen. I promise."

When he looked over at her, Tess brought her arm up in a flash and pointed ahead. "Ben, look."

He spun his neck forward. There was a red pickup truck sitting at a thirty-degree angle on the side of the road, with its hood open. Wisps of smoke drifted upward, curling out of the engine compartment and into the air.

A wiry man, wearing a bright orange baseball hat, shot them a piercing look as they drove past. His cap had been twisted to the side in such a way that the bill stuck out over his left ear, making it look like he had a duck sitting on top of his head.

"Ben, maybe we should stop and—"

"No way. We keep going," Ben said, pressing on the accelerator. "Like you said. My number one focus right now is to get us to the cabin. Somewhere safe. I've had enough of this bullshit."

"You and me both, cousin," Tess said, sitting silent for a good minute after that. Then her tone lightened, as if she had become a different person. "I wonder what's the deal with everyone having car problems? Seems like it's happening everywhere."

Ben snorted a fake laugh, not wanting to follow her down that path. If he did, guilt might crawl into his chest and make him turn around and go back to help some random guy in an orange hat he didn't know. "At least he isn't pinned under the truck."

"Yeah, that was intense. Plus that guy, Jack. He was really something."

"Yeah, he was. Maybe your new boyfriend will come along and help that guy back there. Seems to be how he rolls. You know, Good Samaritan and all."

"I'm pretty sure Jack's on a train by now. Or headed to one. That's the gist of what I think he meant when he showed me his ticket."

Since she wasn't getting his hints, he decided to change the subject. "Hey, I just remembered. We never got any food."

"That's because you were in a super big hurry. Remember? And that place was super slooooooow."

"Uh yeah, but that still doesn't change the fact that I'm starving."

"Probably a good thing we didn't eat there. From what I could tell, the food was nasty," she said, changing her tone to one of amusement. "Rhino ass nasty."

"Seriously? Now you're using one of my lines?"

She shrugged. "Just tired, I guess."

"Still doesn't change the fact that I need food. I'm gonna hop back onto the freeway and see if we can find some place with a drive-thru."

What he really wanted to say was, *Now come on, Tess, tell me what happened. Stop. Stalling. And. Tell. Me. About. Russia.* But he held his tongue, knowing it wouldn't get him anywhere. He knew from experience, she was even more stubborn than him. Especially when she was tired.

Ben took a left onto the next side road and headed for the freeway.

He floored the gas pedal as soon as he reached the on-ramp, merging into a trickle of traffic.

Ben smiled as more words arrived on his tongue. "Here we come, you fat-filled, gut-busting, food of deliciousness. Some form of dead animal on a plate, with a heaping pile of fries. And pickles."

When Tess didn't respond, he looked over to find her holding a blank stare. She sat that way for a good two minutes, looking ahead at what appeared to be nothing.

He kept silent, figuring she'd had enough. Of him. Of the Russians. Of everything.

When a sign came into view with stenciling that indicated a multitude of food choices were available at the next exit, he pointed at it. "Hey, Tess. Bingo."

She still didn't respond, so he jerked the wheel to the right, changing lanes, then zoomed down the off-ramp.

The sudden movement must've shaken Tess from her thoughts, because she blinked a few times and sucked in a deep breath.

Then, out of the blue, she said, "Finally, food. I think maybe I could eat the ass end out of a—"

"Elephant?" Ben quipped, hoping to lighten the tension and make up for his earlier pushiness.

She laughed. "Sure, that too."

Ben turned at the stop sign and headed into an area that would have made the rest of the planet think they had died and gone to fast food heaven.

All along the street were signs touting every kind of burger, taco and chicken stand imaginable.

Ben couldn't hold back a smile. "Now this is what I'm talking about. What do you want?"

"I don't care. You choose."

* * *

Once they'd eaten and gotten back in the Jeep, Ben drove them out of the parking lot and turned, heading toward the highway.

Before they made it to the first intersection, Tess said, "So you asked me earlier if there were any survivors at the Center…"

Actually, he didn't ask her that specific question, but he wasn't about to correct her. "Yeah, but it sounded like you didn't want to talk about it."

"Well, I do now."

"Okay, I'm listening."

"I guess there could be. People alive, I mean. But not a single person I know made it to the Embassy, which is where anyone who made it out would have gone. At least I thought they would have. Then again, the Russians attacked the Embassy, too."

"What? How? Embassies are off limits," Ben said. "I thought that was the law."

She shook her head, then shrugged. "Not that the rules would ever stop the Russians, right?"

"Something major must have gone down. That kind of stuff doesn't just happen."

"I really don't know, but from what I could see, only four Embassy employees survived the attack. The same four who helped me escape."

"At least someone did. I can't even imagine."

"We barely got out of Moscow on this helicopter. This one guy, Stan—funny as hell, had a huge mustache and chewed gum like he owned stock in Wrigley—he was pretty much in charge."

"Huge mustache, huh? Like some porn star from the 70s."

Tess continued, apparently ignoring his joke. "If it weren't for him, I would've died. Right then and there. Well, Stan and—"

"—and what?"

"More like who. Dom—one of my older students at the Center—he's the reason I got away from the Russians and made it to the Embassy. Totally saved me."

"Sounds like you have a lot of friends over there."

"Well, I did," Tess said in a downtrodden tone. "Dom and I kept out of sight in one of the upper rooms while the soldiers started searching the Center. That's when Dom diverted them, giving me a chance to escape."

"Just you?"

"Well, yeah, he's Russian so they escorted him out of the building as a citizen. That's when I made a run for it. But if he hadn't given himself up like that, they would've shot us both for sure. Actually—" she said before pausing. "I was shot. In the leg."

"What?"

"The bullet just grazed me, though. Then I hit my head on this big, ugly dumpster after I jumped out of a window on the top floor. I guess I passed out when I hit my head. Don't really remember for sure. Dom found me and took me to some crazy biochemist guy, who fixed me up."

It took Ben a few seconds to process all the information. "What the fuck, Tess?"

"Huh?"

"Don't give me 'huh.' It's not okay that you haven't told me *any* of this."

"Then you're really going to be upset about everything that went down in Turkey."

"Turkey? What the hell happened there?"

"A whole bunch of stuff. It's almost too much to believe."

"More Russians?"

"And then some. I don't even know where to begin."

"Well, we've got plenty of time, so start at the beginning. And don't leave out a single detail."

CHAPTER 18

"Wait a minute. Are you telling me some Russian guy got into one of the buildings at the Air Force base in Turkey? Past all that security? How?"

"Beats me. But it doesn't change the fact that it did happen."

"You could've been killed."

"Oh believe me, he tried. A lot of Airmen died that day."

"This is fuckin' nuts."

"To say the least."

Ben shook his head, then yawned.

Tess followed suit. "Don't do that. It's contagious."

"I hate to admit it, but I'm exhausted. We either stop for gallons of coffee or find someplace to crash for the night."

"Even though an espresso sounds like heaven right now, I think we better opt for a motel."

Four miles later, the lights from a Motel 6 sign glowed bright against the dark sky.

Ben glanced over at Tess. "What do you think? It's not the Ritz."

"Might as well. I don't think we're going to find a better place."

Ben drove to the front of the building and put the Jeep in park. He got out and headed for the glass front door protecting the motel's office, seeing a cute young girl inside, standing behind the check-in desk. She had blonde hair with purple streaks, looking half asleep as she slumped forward with her elbows on the counter.

Her top showed off her cleavage, giving him hope that the rest of her was just as nice. He could use a little diversion right about now. The kind involving a steamy roll in the sheets, followed by a curt *get the hell out of my room* comment.

He ran his fingers through his hair, then gave his armpits a covert sniff as he approached, deciding on which version of Ben should talk to her. Smooth Ben with a deep voice. Or annoyed Ben, acting completely disinterested in her, as if she wasn't hot. Either way, she was worth chasing, at least for a bit.

As he reached for the handle on the lobby door, a hunched, unshaven man came out of nowhere and tore out of the door, cursing something under his breath.

"Hey, watch it," Ben said, jumping out of the way. That's when he realized the glass door would have smashed into his face if he hadn't reacted so quickly.

The guy furrowed his forehead, mumbled something intelligible, then stomped off toward a rusted, brown-colored minivan with a sizeable dent in its front fender.

Ben stared at the litany of conspiracy stickers decorating the side panel of the vehicle. The first one said *Aliens Live Among Us.* The second one touted something about *Project MKUltra* and the CIA. He stopped reading after the next one that had big, bold letters in red: *It's all fake news. Don't get brainwashed.*

"It takes all kinds," Ben said before turning and looking back at Tess. He could see Wilma hovering at full attention from the back seat, her nose resting on Tess' shoulder.

Tess rolled the window down and leaned half of her torso out. "Do you want me to come with you?"

"Nah, I'm good. Be right out." Ben resumed his trek and went inside, eyeballing the chick with the ample assets.

The girl sprang to life, standing erect as she flicked her hair. "Good evening. How can I help you?"

His eyes found her name tag, hovering just above the promised land. It looked as if the letters had been written with a black magic marker: *Samantha*.

Ben chose his smooth, deep voice. "I need a couple of rooms for me and my cousin out there."

She leaned to the side and looked past him. "Your cousin?"

He nodded, wondering why he decided to tell this girl about Tess being his cousin. It's not like she needed to know. "Problem is, my credit cards don't seem to be working. Can I pay in cash?"

"Must be a full moon or something," Samantha said.

"What do you mean?"

"You are the third person tonight to have credit card issues."

He held up his wallet. "That's why God invented cash."

"Cash? Who pays with cash anymore?"

"Well, I do," he said, opening the fold of his wallet.

"Look, dude. This is like only my second day. I really don't know about taking cash. And of course my manager left early tonight and he's not answering any of my text messages. Which figures, right?"

"Yep, figures. What did the others do?"

"What others?"

"The ones whose cards weren't working."

"I don't know. Went to the next place or something. I told them to get lost. We only take cards. You know, in case you people decide to wreck the place. Gotta have some way to make you pay for the damages."

"Tell you what, Sam," Ben said, pausing to make it more dramatic. He shifted his weight and leaned forward onto the check-in counter, giving the Motel 6 employee a flirtatious smirk.

"It's Samantha," the employee said in a harsh tone. "My name is Samantha. Not Sam. Or Sammie, or babe, or anything like that."

"Sorry. Samantha." He straightened to an upright stance, realizing this girl could not be smooth-talked. "What if I give you the full amount for the night, plus a little extra to cover any incidentals. Would that work?"

She folded her arms, looking defiant.

Ben continued, not willing to give up. "Please. Do me a solid this one time. It's been a long day and we just need to get some sleep. I'll throw in an extra fifty for you. Go do your nails tomorrow or get a massage or whatever."

"For one room, or two?"

"Ah, let's make it one. Need to save some cash."

She paused, then unfolded her arms. "Fine. I just hope this doesn't get me fired. The room costs sixty-five plus tax."

"Just make sure it's got double beds," he said, giving her a hundred dollar bill. "This should cover any extras. Okay?"

"Yep, but what about the other fifty?"

He gave her three more twenties, tucking them in her outstretched hand.

She gave him what looked like a fake smile, then handed him a key. It was attached to a stick the size of a full grown cucumber. "Room eleven, around back. Next to the dumpster."

"The dumpster?"

"All I have in a double."

"Figures."

"Is that it? Cause I have work to do."

"That's it, thanks."

"Uh-huh. Just don't make me regret it."

Ben made quick steps toward the entrance, and then swiveled back in her direction. "Oh, and one more thing. Is it okay to have a dog in the room? She won't be a prob—"

"Oh my God, don't say another word. Just go," Samantha said after sticking her fingers in her ears.

Ben bit his lip to stop from laughing at the hottie who had obvious people issues. He waited a second longer, watching the girl prance back and forth behind the desk with her hands covering her ears, looking as though someone had just stolen her lunchbox.

243

The moment Ben stepped outside, he dangled the key so Tess could see it.

She responded with a thumbs-up.

That's when Ben caught sight of the hunched-over, mumbling man from a few minutes earlier—the one driving the van with the stickers all over it. He walked in tight circles around the vehicle, with his head down and his lips moving.

Before Ben could take another step, the man stopped his hike and pointed at him. "Repent, sinner."

"Sure, whatever dude," Ben mumbled, wanting Crazy Larry, or whatever his name was, to just go away. You never know when a man like that might think he can cast fire and demons down from the heavens and try to interrupt your day.

Ben's lips continued as he walked on a direct line to the Jeep, maintaining his low tone. "Maybe it's time to put that straitjacket back on, buddy. For everyone's sake."

Ben was about to get in the Jeep when he felt something wrap around his bicep and pull, spinning him around.

Crazy Larry stood a few inches in front of Ben, his eyes burning a hole into him.

That's when the guy said, "It's the end of the world."

Ben wasn't sure he heard the man correctly. "The what?"

"You'll see. The end is coming. It's here. It's now. They'll be here in full force. Tomorrow."

Ben shoved him and raised a fist. "Back the fuck off or so help me God, I'll beat the crazy right out of you."

The fire in the man's eyes vanished in a heartbeat, then he turned and cruised back to the van, mumbling the entire way with his arms flailing away.

Ben hopped into the driver's seat and locked the car doors with the touch of a button near the handle.

"Uh, nutjob alert," Tess said, her voice holding a hint of nervousness.

"Ya think? Let's get to the room."

"And lock the door before he follows us."

Room eleven was around back, just like Samantha had said. Right next to the dumpster that was overflowing with trash, diapers and an old couch that someone had tossed into it.

Ben could already smell the rankness wafting in the air. "Figures."

Ben hoped they had installed curtains to block out the brightness from the street light in the alley nearby, its intensity beaming across the area.

He parked, then got out and slung two duffle-style bags over his shoulder that he had tucked in the back seat. He looked at Tess. "I don't want to leave anything in the car. Not with Beelzebub running around loose out here. Will you grab Wilma's stuff for me?"

"Sure thing."

Ben clicked his tongue and the Shepherd darted to his left side. He took the key on the giant stick and opened the door, fantasizing about a good night's sleep.

When he walked inside, the overpowering odor of coconut slammed into his nose. It was mixed with ammonia and seemed to permeate the entire room. He turned his head away in disgust.

"They must have dumped a whole bucket of cleaner in here," Tess said, her nostrils reacting as well.

"Figures," he said, pushing the Jeep's lock button on the remote a few times until the alarm chirped. Then he put the security-entry-latch across the door.

"Which bed you want?" she asked, standing between the two.

"I'll take the one next to the window."

"Cool," she said. "Don't forget to text your dad. Somebody needs to know where we are."

"Right. Bum-fuck-Egypt," Ben said, sliding onto the bed with his butt back against the headboard. "Figures."

He took his cell phone out of his pocket, entered his passcode, and then tapped the green text message box. He typed in his message:

Dad - Have Tess. Everything is fine. Just crossed into Oregon. Crashing at a motel for the night. Will text again once we hit Seattle.

CHAPTER 19

Tess tried for over an hour to fall asleep. Regardless of how exhausted her body felt, the thoughts screaming in her mind would not shut up. It was as if someone was holding a convention in her brain, complete with someone on the drums, banging the cymbals to beat hell.

"You asleep?" she whispered across the room to Ben.

"Huh? What?" Ben mumbled. "Something wrong?"

"Yeah, no, just having a hard time falling asleep, that's all."

Ben groaned, stretched, and rolled over onto his back, then brought the pillow up and around and laid it over his face. "Maybe Beelzebub put a curse on you or something."

"Oh yeah, probably has one of those little voodoo dolls, too. At least I got in a shower. Might have been the best one ever. Shower shoes would've been nice, though, especially with the eight-legged critter living in it. I hate sharing my space."

"Yeah, tell me about it. Don't miss those shower shoes, though. Swore I'd never use them again since my stint in the military."

"I can only imagine."

Ben turned again, this time onto his side, tucking the pillow under his head in a pinching maneuver. "Let's get some sleep, Tess. Long day tomorrow."

Tess knew he was right and decided not to respond. She stared at the ceiling for what seemed like an hour, admiring the faint outline to everything in the room, courtesy of the light trickling in through the crack in the curtains.

She twiddled her thumbs for a few more minutes, then her mouth took over on its own, releasing a string of words she couldn't stop. "Ben, you still awake?"

"No."

"What time is it?"

249

"Time for some shuteye already. Go to sleep."

"I know this is going to sound weird, but I think your dad knew something was going to happen in Moscow."

Ben sat up and peered over at her, his hair sticking up at odd angles. "Why would you say that?"

"I just can't stop thinking about the Russian attack. He left me an urgent message to call him right before it happened. Right before. Then, when I got to the American Embassy, Stan and the others were waiting for me. Me, not someone else. They said your dad reached out to them and told them I was coming and to wait for me. He's the one who arranged for them to get me out of Moscow."

"Are you sure all that wasn't after the shit hit the fan? Not before?"

"No, it started before. I'm sure of it. Why else would he leave me that message to call *before* the attack on the American Center? He never just calls and certainly would never leave an urgent message like that, unless something was wrong."

"What did he say when you talked to him?"

"See, that's the thing. I tried to call, but the phones weren't working. Not my cell phone or the Center's phones. Everything was out."

"Figures," Ben said, flopping back onto the bed and burying his face in the pillow again. "Or, he just wanted to talk to you about something else."

"A coincidence?"

"Yep."

"I suppose it's possible, but I'm not sure what else would be urgent like that out of the blue. Just seems—odd, that's all."

"Well, lots of things are *odd* right now."

"Anyway, it's been nagging at me and I needed to talk about it."

"Sure, I get it. But I'll tell you what. If you go to sleep right now, then I promise we'll give him a good grilling when we get back. Not that it's going to do any good, since he'll only tell us what he wants us to hear, if anything. But we can try. Deal?"

"Deal. Sorry to keep you awake. Night," Tess said as a faint whimper came from Wilma, who was curled into a ball on the floor in the corner.

About a minute after the Shepherd's steady breathing calmed the room, a booming crash rocketed

251

off the walls, knocking Ben off the bed and onto the carpet.

Tess screamed, then stumbled to her feet, which in turn, sent Wilma into a barking fit, both of them bolting to Ben's side.

"What the hell was that?" Ben asked.

Tess opened the drapes. A mass of flames filled the building behind them, in the direction of the lobby. "The motel's on fire!"

"What?"

"Yeah, hurry. We gotta get out of here." Tess threw on some clothes and put on her shoes.

Ben did the same.

The three of them were out of the room in mere seconds and tore around the end of the building and out front.

They could see the lobby—what was left of it.

It was on fire with a brown minivan parked in the middle of it. Someone must have driven through the front glass window, leaving the back half of the van sticking out from the building.

"Shit," Ben said, pulling Wilma closer with the leash. "That's where she sits."

"Who?"

252

"Samantha. The girl who was working—you know, the one at the front desk when I checked in."

"We need to call for help."

Ben gave her his cell phone and the leash just as the hunched man from earlier tumbled out of the double doors on the back of the van. He rolled to the ground in a swirl of smoke, coughing.

Tess dialed 9-1-1. "Come on, answer."

A female's voice came across the phone's speaker. "9-1-1. What's your emergency?"

"A man drove his car into the Motel 6 off the Harney exit. Everything is on fire. We need help. Hurry!"

"Hold on. I'm dispatching emergency crews to that location," the woman said. A few seconds later, she continued. "Are you in a safe location?"

"Yeah, but we need help. Now."

"Crews are on their way. Is anyone hurt?"

"Uh, I don't know. There are flames everywhere," Tess hollered into the phone just as the device vibrated and chimed. She glanced down at the display and saw the battery indicator. It was on zero percent. "Damn it." She looked at Ben. "Your battery just died."

"Shit, must not have plugged it in all the way."

"We need to do something, Ben."

Ben nodded, clenching his teeth. "What if Samantha was at her desk? I need to get in there."

He took a step forward, but Tess grabbed him, pulling him back. "No, it's too dangerous. We have to wait for the fire department."

Just then, the minivan driver forced himself to his feet, still coughing. He turned and stuck his arm back into his van, holding for a beat, then pulled his hand out. That's when Tess noticed something red dangling from his fingers.

Tess pointed. "Is that a gas can?"

"Get back," Ben shouted, stretching his arms out to the side. He walked back several steps, driving Tess and Wilma in reverse along with him.

Motel guests streamed out of their rooms and into the parking lot, forming a makeshift circle not far from their position.

A man with his hair plastered to the side of his head came out of his room to the right, still wearing his pajamas, and went to a VW Bug. He opened the driver's door and shouted, "Screw this." Once he got into the car, he revved the engine and fired it into reverse. It only took seconds to tear out of the lot, squealing tires the entire way.

There was a jumble of voices as other guests huddled a few feet away. Two of them were gray-haired men who seemed to be standing with three college-aged women.

"Somebody needs to do something," one of old guys barked.

Tess went to answer the man, but he had already spun in the opposite direction and run toward the rooms at the far end of the inn.

"Where's he going?" Tess asked whomever might be listening. When Ben didn't answer, she knew he wasn't paying attention.

She returned her focus to the lobby and saw the van driver put the fuel can on the ground and unzip his jacket, then take several steps toward the blaze. It looked as though he was about to head into the fire but stopped and peered back at Tess. He opened his jacket wide, his eyes as fierce as a lion's.

"What's that?" she said, her focus locked on a tangle of wires around his torso.

"That's a bomb! Run!" Ben yelled as the van driver spun on his heels and ran into the flames.

Ben grabbed Tess and pulled her back, leading her and the dog into a dash away from the lobby.

Three strides into her sprint, there was a massive explosion, the compression wave smashing into her back. The impact sent Tess airborne, twisting her in the air like piece of paper in the wind.

Before she could gather her thoughts, her body crashed into the asphalt, landing first on her side, then rolling in a tumble. The side of her head hit next, as her body careened out of control, bouncing and somersaulting, eventually coming to a stop.

She was desperate to lift her head and look for Ben and Wilma, but she couldn't find the energy. That's when her vision ran into a fuzzy blur, right before her mind shut off, smothering her in darkness.

CHAPTER 20

Jack checked the bandages on his neck to make sure they were secure before he got out of the extended cab F150 truck and swung the passenger side door closed.

He wondered what the State of Utah had in store for him. Granted, he was only an hour inside the sprawling border, but he couldn't help but feel something was new. Or different. Maybe both.

Either way, his gut was telling him that he may have just found the glimmer of hope he needed to become the man he wanted to be.

Perhaps a new state line represented the idea of starting over, as if each new locale offered him a welcome reprieve.

From himself.

From his life.

From his past.

Or it was due to the woman who had given him a ride? A woman who stopped on her own and asked if he needed a lift and did so without any provocation from his end. She just pulled over on the highway and asked a total stranger if he needed help.

Amazing stuff, given the state of the world and its propensity to unleash evil on even the nicest of people. Sometimes with him at the helm.

Jack leaned on the edge of the open truck window, giving the attractive redhead behind the wheel a wide smile. "Thanks for the lift, Elsa. Saved me a pile of walking, that's for sure."

"Not a problem, Jack."

"If you hadn't stopped—"

"Don't mention it. Happy to help," she replied.

"Nobody ever stops. Not for a guy like me. I don't know how I will ever be able to repay you."

"You can start by telling me your name."

Jack wasn't sure why she was asking unless she thought he was lying earlier when he told her. "It's Jack, like I said before."

"Your last name, silly. In case we ever meet again type thing."

He couldn't give her his real surname, not after abandoning his old life not that long ago. He was still being hunted by those he used to run with. Nobody ever left that group, and certainly not like he did.

Jack ran a quick search of his memories, deciding on a new name to use. One that a cheerful young girl named Tess helped him find while sitting in a roadside diner.

"It's Bunker. Jack Bunker."

"From California, right?"

"Yes, ma'am. LA. Everything I told you is true."

"I know it is. I have a real sense about people."

"Which is why you stopped," he said in a matter-of-fact-tone, wondering if she would have stopped if she had known who he really was.

She smiled and held her gaze on him.

He did the same, not wanting this chance meeting to end. He, too, had a sense about people. However, that sense usually involved knowing whether or not the guy standing across from him was going to make the first move and pull a weapon.

Elsa was armed, too, just not with the type of armaments he was used to defending himself from. Her curves were amazing; so was her smile.

If keeping a low profile hadn't been his priority, he would've liked to have gotten to know this svelte, green-eyed beauty a whole lot better. She had a quiet way about her, choosing her words carefully, as if they were more valuable than a bar of gold.

If someone had asked him to describe her in the fewest words possible, it would have been *always in control.*

Elsa was not like most of the women he'd met in his lifetime—the kind who had an agenda—always pestering and then judging, looking for an angle to work him.

He knew from experience that everyone wants something. More so when you joined forces with the last group of men Bunker ran with.

"So this place is yours?" he asked, making a sweeping motion with his hand at the immense spread of fields and horse corrals. He wasn't sure how big her farm was, but it seemed to go on forever.

"Yup. All mine. It's been in my family for almost—"

Elsa cut her words off when a black Cadillac roared over the incline ahead, tearing across the dirt road at a high rate of speed.

It angled to the right a few degrees, aiming its chrome grille at the front of her truck. A few seconds later, the Caddy slid to a stop, about twenty feet away.

Two men got out of the vehicle, one of them wearing a form-fitting tank top and jeans, while the other sported a three-piece suit, both men waving their hands as a cloud of dust settled to the ground around them.

"Who the hell are these guys?" Bunker asked before taking in a slow breath to calm the reaction building inside his chest.

Elsa shook her head. "Shit. Like clockwork."

Tank top guy, who Bunker thought was the spitting image of a young Lou Ferrigno, planted his feet shoulder-width apart and folded his hands together in front of his belt buckle. His biceps twisted like bulging cords of rope, pushing the limits of his skin to the point of eruption.

"Let me guess. Your farm?" Bunker asked, knowing it was none of his business, but the hairs on the back of his neck had other ideas.

"Developers," Elsa said in an even tone. "They're relentless."

Bunker studied their body stance and posture, then took in the size of their chests. "Since when do developers pound iron like that?"

"Well, they're not just developers."

"I think I'll hang around for a bit."

"Nah, I got this. It's the same thing every month. First they tack on another zero, then I say thank you but no. They'll huff and puff like they're going to do something, but eventually they'll leave. They always do."

Bunker held his tongue as a flash of images roared through his mind, each one awash in a sea of rage.

If this encounter had taken place before he went on this walkabout to find the new version of himself, he would have already been in go-mode, tearing into these men without a second thought.

Action over reaction was what his former self was all about, but the new Jack Bunker had to reboot, taking a less obvious route when it came to situations like this. That was the promise he'd made to himself before he set out on this voyage to nowhere in particular.

Regardless of his new approach, he could always tell what was on an adversary's mind by peering into the man's eyes. It was a skill he'd learned after hundreds of street fights and several tours in active red zones.

The eyes are the key to everything—they tell you the immediate future, more so when dealing with mouth breathers who prioritize gym time over everything else.

His old drill instructor in the Corps liked to call it 'myopic intention'—a state of mind where a brute's next move is in direct opposition to common sense.

It usually showed itself right at the moment when his patrol faced down yet another suicide bomber. It never seemed to end. One after another, the radicals would appear with one thing on their minds—take out as many as they could before releasing the dead man's switch.

Yet myopic intention wasn't all Bunker detected with these two guys.

Their look of overconfidence was on full display, giving him the advantage, albeit a small one. It made up for the sun being at their backs instead of his, their shadows casting a line straight and true at Bunker's feet.

He knew exactly who they were, but they had no idea who he was. All it would take was one quick jab of his hand to their throats and they'd be breathing through a tube for the rest of their days.

When the second man locked eyes with him, Bunker moved his hand to the sheath that held his Ka-Bar knife. His other hand went into his pocket, checking for the position of the Benchmade folding knife his father had given him a long time ago.

In reality, knives gave Bunker more comfort than actual protection, but they did offer a couple of important advantages over a firearm.

First, they never stove-piped a round in the chamber. And second, they never ran out of ammo. Two important aspects that some of his former brethren seemed to forget.

Suit Guy removed his jacket and folded it over his left arm using a creasing technique, confirming what Bunker already suspected about the guy's physique.

The man's commitment to pushing weights was equal to that of Tank Top guy standing next to him, just with a better fashion sense mixed in.

That's when Bunker spotted it—a Colt 1911 hugging Suit Guy's right hip, sitting in a quick-release holster. The same .45 sidearm many of his fellow Marines carried as their preferred service weapon.

"Well, that's new," Elsa said, sounding less confident than before.

"Figured as much," Bunker said in a matter-of-fact tone.

"It'll be okay, Jack. Let me handle it," Elsa replied, opening the driver's door of the vehicle. She stepped onto the gravel road, looking calm and determined, before closing the door behind her.

The two strangers approached with methodical steps as she advanced.

Elsa stopped her feet when they did, all of them now standing just beyond the front bumper of the truck. "I haven't changed my mind since your last visit, gentlemen."

"Who's this clown?" Tank Top asked, pointing a sausage finger at Bunker.

Else shook a finger at him. "None of your damn business, Tony."

Bunker moved in next to Elsa, deciding to keep his hands ready and mouth closed, needing to gather more intel and assess.

Tony pointed at Bunker's playing-card sized bandages on his neck. "Looks like dumbass here needs a refresher course in shaving."

"Yeah, with a chainsaw," Suit Guy added.

"What's with the gun, Sam?" Elsa asked Suit Guy.

Sam brought his eyes to her. "Clock's ticking, Elsa. Uncle told me to tell you this is your last chance. After this, things escalate."

Else leaned the top half of her body forward with her hands on her hips. "I already told you, there's nothing to talk about. *I. Am. Not. Selling. My. Farm.* Not to you. Not to your Uncle Clive. Not to anyone."

"We're not playing, Elsa," Tony said.

Elsa moved a step toward them, but Bunker stopped her with an arm grab.

266

She shook her head. "Please, Jack. I've got this."

He ignored her plea and took a few steps forward to position himself in front of her, corralling her with his forearms, then walking her back in a reverse shuffle of his feet.

"You heard the lady," Bunker said to Sam, before turning his attention to Tony. "The answer is no."

"This ain't your business, *Jack*," Tony said as if Bunker's first name brought him amusement.

Bunker ignored the man's dig. "You boys run along home now and go play with your peckers, before you both get hurt."

"Fuck off, asshole," Sam said, his hand moving to his waistline and resting near the top of the holster. "This is between her and us."

"Not today," Bunker said with his jawline pressing out more than normal. "I'd suggest you both vacate the premises."

"I suggest you shut the hell up," Tony replied, repositioning his feet in an even wider stance.

Sam touched his free hand to Tony's shoulder, then brought his gaze to Bunker. "We're here to work out a deal and that's what we're going to do."

Before Bunker could respond, Elsa pushed forward against his back and nestled in next to him, bringing her lips to his ear. "Jack, please. Don't."

Bunker brought his eyes to hers, wanting to take a read on her tone. It wasn't calm like before. This time her words carried a hint of unsteadiness. Not at all surprising given the circumstances.

"You heard her, Jack," Tony said. "Time to make like a tree and get the fuck outta here."

"We're just about done with this little game," Sam added.

"Trust me, boys. This is no game," Bunker said, nudging Elsa behind him once again. He unclipped the leather snap keeping his knife in its sheath, not bothering to conceal his actions. In fact, just the opposite; he was hoping to send a message.

"Didn't your old man teach you nothing? You never bring a knife to a gunfight," Sam said in a snide voice, before turning his attention to Tony. "Gotta love them pig stickers."

268

"And the morons who carry them," Tony quipped before leaning his head back and letting out a bellowing laugh. After his neck righted itself, one of his hands released from his belt buckle and moved behind his back and stayed there. "Kind of useless, if you ask me."

"Then you're really going to love this," Bunker said, taking the Benchmade folding knife from his pocket. He used his thumb to engage the auto-assist release mechanism, setting the 3.5-inch blade free in a 180-degree snap.

"Really? You think two blades are going to make a difference?" Sam asked, flaring his eyes.

"Two blades for two assholes," Bunker said.

Tony shook his head at Bunker then turned his focus to Sam. "He's even dumber than I thought, cousin."

At that moment Sam's face ran white with numbness as he took in what looked like a purposeful breath and held it.

When Sam tightened his eyes, Bunker knew it was time.

All in one motion, Bunker pulled his Ka-Bar from the sheath and whirled around to Elsa, pushing her down with the heel of his hand.

She flew in the air, landing on her butt in a flop next to the rear passenger door as Bunker completed his spin. He brought the Ka-Bar knife up and into a throwing position, using his momentum to set it free at Sam.

It zipped at the man's neck like a speeding dart, just as Sam brought his sidearm into firing position.

Tony was now standing a bit sideways, with his free hand up in front of his face and his other hand pulling something out from his beltline along the back, as Bunker dropped into a backwards roll.

A gunshot rang out, probably from Sam, ripping through the air with the sound of thunder.

Bunker completed his reverse somersault with adrenaline fueling his body, then swung the driver's door open in a flash, positioning himself between Elsa and the armrest.

He didn't have time to check to see if he'd taken a bullet as two more shots rang out, pelting the steel frame of the truck's door.

"Motherfucker!" Tony yelled before three additional rounds impacted the vehicle.

When Bunker saw a man's shadow creep forward under the door, he was thankful it was only one pair of legs, not two, coming in from the left where Tony had been standing. It was time to act before Tony worked his way to the side for an open shot, assuming what the man pulled out from his beltline was a handgun.

Bunker flipped the Benchmade knife around in his hand, wrapping his fingers around the blade, then sucked in a quick breath to steel himself. He brought his head and shoulders up and fired the knife at Tony, hoping he'd catch Tony off guard.

It was at that moment Bunker caught a glimpse of the results from his first knife throw. Sam was down and bleeding from the Ka-Bar sticking into his neck, lying on his back in a pool of blood.

Bunker dropped behind the door once again as three more rounds went off, two of which hit the door in front of him.

He looked down and watched for changes below the door. A moment later, the shadow caved in on itself, vanishing from view as a thud was heard.

Bunker didn't hesitate, shooting to his feet and taking off for Tony. He'd expected to see that the Benchmade had impaled Tony somewhere near the middle of his face, but that's not what his eyes reported.

The knife was lying a few feet away without any blood on it, yet Tony was down on his back and not moving. The only thing Jack could figure was that it must have dented the thick skull of Tank Top boy, stunning him.

Bunker finished his approach and hopped onto Tony's chest and pulled his fist back as rage filled his body with strength.

He unleashed a strike, smacking the man's nose in a resounding crack.

Blood shot out in spurts and, a moment later, soaked the man's lips and mouth in red.

Bunker let out a roar as he pulled his arm back for another punch, planning to beat Tony until the very last breath left the man's body.

Before he could unleash hell, a pressure landed on his arm from behind.

"That's enough, Jack," Elsa said, her hands wrapped around his wrist. She pulled at him, cradling his hand in the softness of her chest.

He let the strength in his arm wither, then rolled back to his feet and got off Tony, with Elsa still holding onto him.

Bunker looked down at her with a steady gaze. "You know they're never gonna stop. Not until you're dead or they are."

She released him, letting her fingers dangle across his skin as if maintaining contact was all-important. "Honestly, I never thought that until now."

"Well, obviously something has changed. They just tried to kill us both," Bunker said, walking over and picking up his folding knife. He pressed the release mechanism, then folded it up and stowed it in his pocket.

He stood over Tony, debating which version of himself should finish the conversation with this innocent woman. He turned to her. "I should really deal with this guy while I have the chance. It's never wise to leave loose ends. Not loose ends like these two. Trust me when I say that. I've seen it a million times."

"This isn't like them at all," Elsa said, obviously not hearing what Bunker had just said.

"Like I said, something has changed. We need to act now, not react later. Once they start shooting, there's no going back. It's kill or be killed. Simple as that."

She didn't respond, only standing like a statue.

Bunker went to her and grabbed her arm, making sure she was paying attention to what he had to say. "Where is this uncle of theirs?"

Elsa shook her head, looking at the two bodies on the ground for a moment, then back at Bunker. "No, I'll deal with Clive myself. You should leave, Jack. I need to report this to the Sheriff. I don't want to get you in trouble."

"I need to finish Tony and then go take care of their uncle. Pronto. Otherwise, they'll send more."

"There are no more, Jack. Just these two and Clive. It's a family deal, ever since their feed store went belly-up."

"Feed store?"

"Yes. A small-town thing. Something you wouldn't understand, not when you grew up in a big city like LA. Let me handle this. Otherwise, it's only going to get worse."

"It's already worse, or can't you see that?"

"It'll be fine. This is my town and I know how to handle it. Please, Jack. For your own sake, go. Now. Before you get caught up in all this."

"I'm already caught up in it."

"Not as far as anybody knows."

Bunker pointed at the man who was still breathing, albeit with his eyes closed. "Except Tony."

"It'll be my word against his."

Bunker shook his head. "That's all well and good, but how are you going to explain what happened here?"

"Won't have to. The Sheriff is my brother Lyle. He'll cover for me. I swear. Please, just go. Everything will be okay. I promise."

"Are you sure? Because if I were in your shoes, I would finish this once and for all. Leave no doubt. Otherwise, you're always going to be looking over your shoulder, and that's no way to live. Trust me when I say that. That's a stress nobody should ever have to live with."

"You've done enough, Jack," Elsa said, putting two hands on his chest and giving him a shove. "You need to leave right now and never come back. Please. You need to trust me. I've got this."

CHAPTER 21

Nausea hit Tess like a tsunami. It started in the pit of her gut, then inched its way up her throat. Her eyes watered as she tried to swallow the taste of acid that continued to assault her esophagus.

The queasiness paled in comparison, though, to the stabs of pain ravaging her temples. She figured this is what it would feel like if someone slammed a hammer against the side of her head. "Ben, pull over."

"Again? We're almost to the cabin. I knew you should've gone to the hospital. The EMT at the motel said—"

"Ben!"

"Okay, okay," Ben said as he drove onto the shoulder of the road.

Just before the Jeep came to a full stop, she pushed the passenger side door open and tumbled onto the ground, landing on her knees first.

It took a few seconds, but she finally convinced herself to get up.

Then it happened—she doubled over at the waist and released a stream of vomit from her mouth, splattering a stream of chunks on the rocks by her feet. Tess gagged as she took in air, hurling three more times, each one a bit less than the spew before.

Once she knew the worst was over, she took out a tissue from her pocket and wiped her mouth. "That ferry ride didn't help at all."

"How many times have we ridden that thing and you've never gotten sick before? No, you're barfing up a lung because you have a fuckin' concussion," Ben said.

Tess knew Ben was right, but there was no way in hell she was going to spend another second in a hospital. Or in a helicopter. Or under fire.

She was sick of flying, driving, car troubles, medical problems and most of all—tired of all the questions that kept flashing over and over in her head.

It was like listening to that God-awful song from the movie *Frozen* on repeat.

She needed answers from Ben's dad. And she needed them now.

Tess took in a deep breath and held it, calming the butterflies in her stomach. She got back in the vehicle. "All right, let's get moving. Your dad's probably pacing a hole in the cabin floor by now."

"Yeah, about that—why the cabin? Don't you think that's weird? Why not the house in the city?"

She rolled her eyes, making sure he saw her do it. "You worry too much."

"Well, someone has to. You obviously don't."

"I'm sure he has his reasons."

"That's my point. He always has a reason. For everything. He doesn't take a dump without a plan. If he picked the cabin of all places, then—"

She sighed, feeling her eyelids close a bit on their own. "Look, we just need to do what Ambassador Hudson told us to do, which is meet your dad at the cabin. Anything else is just a waste of time and energy."

"I get it. I get it. You're tired."

"You're damn right I'm tired. In fact, I'm exhausted. How about less talk and more driving."

"Almost there," Ben said before veering left onto an unkempt gravel driveway. The crunch of pebbles under the Jeep's tires popped, shooting debris in all directions.

Ben slowed as they approached the A-frame log cabin.

She raised her focus from the floorboard and took in the scene ahead. The weekend home was an exact replica of the one she'd conjured up from her memories, including the spread of green moss that covered the ground, then wound its way up the bark of the Ponderosa Pines that stood guard across the property.

Ben slowed the Jeep. "Wait, where's Dad's truck?"

"Maybe he's still on his way. It's not like we told him what time we'd be here."

"True," Ben answered, jamming on the brakes and bringing the vehicle to a stop.

"You should shoot him a text. Let him know we're here."

Ben didn't answer, only pushing the driver's side door open and stepping out.

Wilma jumped into the front seat and followed him out, her tail wagging.

After a glance at Ben, who gave Wilma a quick hand wave, Wilma bolted to a nearby tree and marked it as her own with one of her squats.

Tess got out of the Jeep and followed Ben up the steps, where she tilted a terra-cotta pot up and pulled a key from its bottom. She wiped the dirt off before sliding it into the lock and turning it. She pushed the door open, then turned to Ben and gave him a sweeping, Shakespearian-style bow. *"Entrée-vous."*

He went inside, flipped on the light switch and stopped two steps later. "Holy shit. Look at all this stuff."

"What?" she asked, stepping in behind him.

Ben walked forward, heading toward the hallway. "It's like the end of the fucking world in here."

Tess couldn't stop her mouth from dropping open as she ran a count of the canned food boxes, pallets of water bottles, hand-crank flashlights and radios, blankets, first aid kits, walkie-talkies, toilet paper, even several bags of dog food—the piles seemed endless, filling the entire living space. There was even a stack of red book bags inside, the kind that kids use at school.

"Uh, Tess? You should look really come look at this," Ben called out from the study down the hall.

When she arrived in the doorway to the study, her eyes reported at least twenty crates stenciled with black numbers on them. "Good God."

Ben swept his arm from one end of the room to the other, sending a shadow across the floor from the overhead light. He sat down on the corner of the desk, only inches from another lamp sending out a swash of light. "You know what they say, you can never have enough ammunition."

"Apparently."

"Okay, that's it. I'm calling him." Ben pulled out his phone and brought his finger to the screen when the overhead light exploded in a sea of sparks. So did the desk lamp, its reaction just as intense.

Tess ducked and flinched; so did Ben as his cell phone fell out of his hands and crashed into the floor.

"What the hell was that?" she asked, seeing a trail of smoke rising from the metal shroud covering the bulb in the desk lamp.

"I think that was a power surge," he replied, picking up his phone. He pressed a few buttons, then held for a few beats with his eyebrows pinched. "Well, that's not good."

"What?"

"Phone's dead."

"That's what happens when you drop it."

"I'm not so sure about that. I've dropped it a million times and it always worked before."

"Hey, at least you have one. God knows where mine is right now."

He held up the device and shook it at her. "Might as well be a paperweight at this point. Fucking technology. It's great when it works."

Tess wrapped her arms around herself, feeling a chill take over her skin. It had come out of nowhere and she knew it wasn't from the temperature in the room. "Hey, I know your dad said to meet him here, but I'm starting to think maybe this wasn't such a good idea."

Ben seemed to ignore her statement. "Better go check the breaker and see what's what."

Tess grabbed him by the arm as he walked past, turning him sideways. "Hey, did you hear me?"

He pulled away. "Just give me a minute. I'm sure it's just the fuse box."

She followed him down the hallway and back into the main room. The light that was on before was no longer shining.

"Looks like this one's out, too," he said. "I'm going to go reset some breakers, so you stay here and let me know if anything comes back on."

"Okay."

About a minute later, Tess heard him call out from the side of the cabin. "Anything?"

"Nope, nothing."

"How about now?"

"Sorry. No," she answered as Wilma plopped down and began nudging her hand. Tess obeyed the canine's request and began scratching the Shepherd between her ears.

She waited another minute or so for Ben to return from outside.

"Fucking thing is fried. Not sure what's going on," Ben said.

"Can we go now? Like I said before."

He scratched his head. "Hmmm, I wonder why the generator didn't kick on?"

"Seriously, we need to leave."

"Must be out of gas."

"Or maybe everything just fried. Power surge, remember?"

Ben walked to the fridge and opened it. "Well, at least the fridge is empty. One less thing I have to worry about."

Tess checked, but didn't see light leaking out of the fridge before Ben closed its door. "How about we worry ourselves someplace safe. As in not here. Something ain't right, Ben. We need to go."

He stood for a few beats, his eyes locked on hers. "Okay, but first I'm going leave a note for my old man. You know, just in case he shows up. Don't want him to think I fried the electrical in this place or that I never showed up. That's just grief I don't need right now."

"Fine, do what you have to do. But let's get moving."

A few minutes later, they left the cabin and Tess locked the door and put the key back under the pot where she had found it. She went to the Jeep and got in, feeling a wet nose from Wilma brush across the back of her neck.

285

Ben leaned forward and tapped his forehead against the top of the steering wheel in a slow, measured beat.

"What's wrong?"

Ben sat up and grabbed the key sticking out from the ignition. When he turned it, nothing happened. "That's what's wrong."

"Shit. The Jeep, too?"

"Yep. First the lights, then my phone. And now this."

"What the hell is going on?"

"Not sure. But I'm starting to think that was no ordinary power surge."

"Yeah, I think you're right. I guess we're walking back to the ferry?"

"That'll take forever. I have a better idea," Ben answered, pulling at the door latch and stepping out. "Follow me."

Tess and Wilma sprinted in behind him as he headed toward the back of the cabin, where he stopped in front of a wooden shed. A combination lock dangled from the latch on the door.

Ben fiddled with the lock, then opened it and stepped in, disappearing into the darkness inside.

After about thirty seconds of him shuffling around inside and letting a few choice curse words fly, Tess heard a clank of tools hit the floor.

It wasn't long after that when Ben appeared in the doorway, carrying a bike over his shoulder. It was covered in spider webs and most of the paint along the frame had flaked off.

She looked at the flat tire on the back. "Looks like it hasn't been used in a while. I hope you have a pump somewhere."

"Yes, ma'am. There's one inside, if I remember right. At least there used to be."

Tess stuck her head inside the shed but couldn't see much else. "So tell me, is that the only bike?"

"Yep. Just this old beast. You're gonna have to sit on the handlebars. Old school like."

"Great. Just what I need."

"I'm thinking we should grab a few of the items Dad stashed inside. You know, just in case."

"Good thinking. You fill up the tires, while I go grab what we need."

"Use one of those red backpacks inside the door. You'll need to keep your hands free."

"Yeah, tell me about it. I remember how you ride."

"Hopefully, I still remember how."

CHAPTER 22

The relentless bouncing of the mountain bike as it barreled down the rocky trail brought only one thought to Tess's mind—if only she had taken some Advil while she was at the cabin. Assuming her uncle had a stash around there somewhere.

Her brain felt like mush and her back ached. Never mind the permanent bruise developing on her butt from the handlebars.

How the hell she and Ben did this all day long on these dirt roads when they were kids, she had no idea. But at least Wilma was keeping up, running alongside in that casual gallop that dogs seem to do with ease.

"Are we getting close?" she asked, seeing something in the road. "Hey, watch that rock!"

Ben swerved and missed the protrusion, but the sudden weight shift sent her sideways, almost flying off the handlebar. It was all she could do not to fall off, especially with the backpack strapped to her spine.

"Shit, hang on," Ben said, the bike wobbling in a sudden zigzag pattern.

"I'm trying. Maybe slow down a bit?"

"Relax, I got it," he said, finding a straight-line path once again. His peddling slowed.

She lessened the hydraulic grip of her fingers around the metal bar. "Jesus, that was close."

"Thought I lost you there for a second."

"Thanks for slowing down."

"Yep, slow and smooth from here on out. Well, maybe not smooth," he said into her ear using a light, flippant tone.

"I'm glad you think this is funny, but my ass is killing me."

"Just a couple more miles. Then we're there."

A few minutes later, the density of the trees thinned as they neared the bottom of the path. That's when she saw it—a stab of asphalt cutting at a perpendicular angle to their path.

"Is that it?"

"Yep, the main road," Ben said.

"It's about time."

"How's your ass doing? Do we need to take five?"

"I'm good. Keep going. It'll be easier on the pavement."

Tess tucked in her lip and took the pain until they made it to the dock, about two miles later.

"What the hell's going on now?" Ben asked.

"What?"

Ben brought the bike to a halt, then pointed over her shoulder, past a line of cars, many of which sat with their hoods up and driver side door open. "By the ferry, where all those people are."

They both got off and stood together with the dog, who was now panting like a freight train.

"She really needs some water," Tess said, motioning to Wilma.

"Sit, girl," Ben said to Wilma before putting the bike's kickstand down and then digging his hand into the zipper pocket of the backpack.

When he pulled his fingers out, he was clutching Wilma's leash. He clipped it to her harness, then found a water bottle inside the pack and poured some liquid into his hand. He held it under Wilma's nose and let her lap it up.

"Let's go," he said after repeating that same process several times, aiming his feet toward the crowd across the way.

The closer they came to the group the louder the voices grew. People were yelling, even threatening the dock workers.

"You better get me the hell on this ferry," a middle-aged blonde woman said, jabbing her finger into the cashier's face.

At the back of the line, a short, stout man leaned in front of a skinny guy with a serious comb-over.

Skinny man pushed the other and then a shoving match broke out, each one taking turns jamming hands into the other's chest.

"I was only trying to see what was going on," the stout guy said to stickman.

Their old-man fight continued a few more rounds until they both were out of breath and leaning over with hands on their knees.

"Stay here with Wilma. Let me see if I can find out what's happening," Tess said, shoving her thumbs through the straps of her pack. She slid it off and tried to give it to Ben.

He refused to accept it. "No, you stay here. I'll do it."

Tess shook her head. "Not this time. It's my turn. Besides, these people will be nicer to a girl than someone who might come across as threatening."

"I still don't like it."

"Please, let me do this. I'll be fine."

He nodded and took the pack from her, though he didn't seem to like it much.

She avoided the two men at the back who were still gasping for air as she walked to a different guy who was as tall as he was wide. "Excuse me, sir, may I ask you a question?"

The giant never responded.

She tapped him on the shoulder. "Excuse me—"

"Yeah, yeah, yeah. I heard you the first time. What do you want?"

"Well, I was wondering—"

"No, you're not cutting in line, if that's what you think."

"No, that wasn't it at all. I'm just wondering what happened? Why is everyone so amped up?"

"Do you live under a rock or something? The power's out. Everywhere. Where have you been?"

"I figured that was the case, but I wasn't sure."

"Supposedly the ferry isn't working, either. But I think they're lying. It's a conspiracy, if you ask me, where only *certain* people get to ride, if you know what I mean. The kind of people with piles of cash. Not us working stiffs."

"Okay, well—"

The guy grabbed her arm. "Don't think for a minute I buy this whole wondering about stuff excuse. I know why you came over here and I'm not letting it happen. No way. No how."

Ben showed up out of nowhere with Wilma, taking a spot next to her. He pulled the man's hand free from Tess and then bumped chests with the guy. "Look, dude, keep your Goddamn hands off her or you'll be swimming across. You feel me?"

The big guy shoved Ben back a step. "Get out of my face, kid. You and that bitch over there are not getting ahead of me."

"What did you just call her?"

Wilma barked and growled at the guy, while the entire back half of the line turned their attention to Ben from the old guys who were back to shoving each other.

Tess moved in front of Ben. "Don't. He's not worth it."

Tess put her hands on Ben's chest and pushed him away from the group, bringing Wilma along on the leash.

Ben's chin was sticking out and his teeth were clenched when he said, "What's wrong with that guy? He totally pissed me off."

"I thought you were going to stay put."

"I was, but then those guys started up their fight again and I wasn't comfortable letting you deal with all this by yourself."

She continued to escort Ben and the dog away from the others. "Forget these people. We have bigger things to deal with. Did you hear what he said?"

"Oh yeah. I heard him loud and clear. You know, Tess, it's not okay to let people talk to you like that. Or put their hands on you."

"No, not that. Get over it; he's an idiot."

"Still—"

"He said the power's out here too and the ferry isn't working."

"The ferry, too?"

"Yeah, weird right?"

"Then it must all be connected somehow."

"I wonder if it's just here or all over the place?"

"Depends on what it is."

"What do you mean?"

He pointed back the way they came in. "It means, look around. Do you see all those cars over there with their hoods up?"

"Yeah, so?"

"Well, take a minute and think. What would cause all these power surges, cell phones to die, cars to stop working, lights to explode, and a ferry to stop running?"

She thought about it for a good ten seconds, but her mind came up empty.

Ben shook his head, looking frustrated. "It's an EMP, Tess."

"A what?"

"Electromagnetic pulse. It fries everything."

"Seriously?"

"Yeah, must have hit the whole area by the looks of it. I wonder how far it went?"

"You mean like statewide?"

He looked up and stared at the sky. "I think these things are line of sight, though. Usually from a nuke or something?"

"A nuke?"

"I think so, but science really isn't my thing."

She looked around. "Then where's the mushroom cloud?"

"Maybe it was a different kind."

"You mean like new technology?"

"Roger that. We all know they're always working at something."

"Oh yeah. And we're always the last ones to know."

"Regardless of how they did it, the facts seem obvious."

"So what do we do?"

"I think I have an idea," Ben said, turning right and heading up the street toward the shoreline.

Tess followed, seeing a sailboat tethered at the end of the dock. "Seriously?"

"Don't need power for those."

Tess glanced over her shoulder to see if anyone noticed them leaving and decided to follow. She didn't see anyone.

When they arrived at the boat, they found a bearded, scraggy man sitting in a lawn chair, with a beer can in his hand. There was a blue and white cooler sitting next to his right foot.

Ben cleared his throat. "Hey, how you doing?"

The man pointed at the crowd by the ferry. "You might as well turn around right now."

"Please, we just need to get across."

"Not my problem," the man said, looking up at the three of them. "This is my private slip and you're trespassing. I'd advise you to leave. Now."

"We can pay you," Tess said.

"I don't want your money. I just want all of you people to leave me the hell alone."

"A hundred bucks each," Tess said, realizing that others from the ferry must have tried the same thing. She figured they just didn't offer enough. Everyone has their price. Even guys like this.

Ben grabbed Tess's arm and widened his eyes.

She held up a hand and flared an eyebrow, pushing on Ben's chest with light pressure.

"It's like I'm talking to a couple of posts," the man said as he stood up, grabbed his chair and cooler, and stepped onto his boat. "What is it with these people? Don't they understand plain English?"

Tess put out her hands. "Wait, mister, please—"

The old man didn't respond, only talking to himself in a mumble as he readied the boat for an apparent departure, working his rigging lines.

Tess wasn't going to take no for an answer. "Look, our Jeep isn't working. Our cell phone is dead. And I have a headache the size of Cleveland."

"Plus, we have an important meeting with my old man. He's a Senator in Washington," Ben added.

Tess shot a look at Ben, hoping he'd be quiet. Then she turned her focus back to the boatman. "We just need to get across the bay, then we'll be on our way. Please."

The man hesitated for a moment, then shook his head and continued his prep work.

"Really, dude?" Ben asked. "You're just going to leave us here."

"Like I said, not my problem."

Tess took a step forward, adding volume to her words. "Two hundred bucks each. That's got to pique your interest."

The old sailor stood upright, locking his knees and arching his back. "Okay, I'll tell you what—"

Tess took in a breath and held it, waiting to hear if he'd accept her offer.

"Make it five hundred each and I'll consider it."

"A thousand bucks? Seriously?" Ben asked. "Seems a bit steep for a ride across the bay. It's not like you're going to burn any fuel."

"Your math is off, my obnoxious friend. It's fifteen hundred. There's three of you."

Ben threw up his hands. "You're gonna charge us for my dog?"

"Nothing's free in this world, kid, despite what the news wants you to believe. Everything costs somebody something. Especially all that free shit they're always promising you for your vote."

Ben dragged Tess out of earshot of the man. "That's too much, Tess."

"What choice do we have?"

The old man cleared his throat. "Hey, you two. I'm shoving off. So what's it gonna be?"

"Still got your ATM card?" Tess asked Ben in a guarded whisper.

"Why? Those won't be working either."

"Assuming the surge wasn't just here."

"That's true. Might have only been localized."

"And if wasn't, he won't know either way."

"Oh, I see where you're going with this. Buys us time," Ben said, opening his wallet and handing her the card.

"It's all about getting to where we need to go and that can't happen unless we get on that boat."

"So we tell him what he needs to hear," Ben said, nodding.

Tess turned to the boat captain and held up the plastic. "I'll tell you what, old man, we'll double the price, if you'll agree to take us right now. No questions asked. Just need to find an ATM machine and we'll pay you three grand in crisp one-hundred-dollar bills. All for just being a decent human being. So what's it going to be?"

The old man smiled and waved at Tess. "Hop on board, my new friends. My name is Marcus."

301

"I'm Tess and this is my good friend Ben."

Ben gave Wilma's leash to Tess. "I'll go grab the bike."

"So tell me, are you two bumping uglies or what?" Marcus asked.

Tess laughed, then shook her head. "No. Just a couple of friends trying to get home."

"Where's home?"

"Seattle. Well, Bell Hill actually."

"That's not exactly across the bay."

"I know. I hope you don't mind. But you'd save us a lot of time, if you could see it in your heart to drop us a little closer to where we need to go."

The boat captain held out his hand to Tess. "For three grand, I can do that. Just make sure that mutt of yours doesn't leave a landmine on my deck."

CHAPTER 23

Elsa watched Deputy Dwayne's patrol car pull away in a spin of its tires, hauling Tony to jail in a flash of red and blue lights.

The man's head was tilted to the right, resting on the side window in the back seat. She couldn't believe he was still woozy. Then again, Jack did hit him hard. Not once, but twice, if the blunt impact from the knife throw counted as the first round.

She turned and stared at the path Jack had taken when he left, wondering how far away the handsome stranger was at this point.

Somewhere out there was a selfless human being. A man who reacted faster than she ever thought possible. A man who helped a near-total stranger, which is what she would consider herself, without any regard for himself.

And to think, all she did was stop and give a random tattooed guy a ride. And now this.

Was it luck that she did?

What would have happened if she hadn't?

Would she be the one lying dead on the road?

In truth, her mind was having a hard time processing the entire situation. Nothing felt real. Not the air around her. Not what her eyes were reporting. And certainly not what she felt in her heart at the moment. Everything seemed like a dream.

Yet the body lying on the road in a pool of its own blood might say differently, wanting to rise up and beat her over the head with the notion of reality.

She waited until her brother finished scribbling something on his incident report before she said, "That's how it happened, Lyle. I swear."

Lyle shook his head, tucking his upper lip under as he closed the clipboard cover and turned to his squad car.

He tossed the paperwork onto the front seat, then closed the door, with the blinking emergency lights highlighting the disappointment on his face. "The coroner might think differently when I call him in."

"How, exactly?"

"Look at you, sis. Who in their right mind is going to believe that a 100-pound woman who grows feed corn for a living got the drop on these guys? With a knife, no less?"

"Like I said, I just got lucky."

"I'd say it was more than luck. Plus, where is the weapon? Normally, we find it at the scene somewhere," he said, raising an eyebrow at her before pointing at the dirt a few yards away. "And then there are those boot prints. Worn soles. Deep impressions. Size 14. Big guy, I take it. Care to explain?"

She stepped forward and wrapped her arms around her brother, betting he would stop his interrogation if she just ignored it. "Thanks for handling this for me."

He hugged her back, letting an exhale linger before he spoke in an even tone. "It's what Dad would have done, when he was Sheriff."

"Still, I owe you."

"The list is getting pretty long, sis."

"I know. Trouble seems to be following me lately."

"That's an understatement. First the incident at the Hobby Barn in town, then at the feed store, and now this?"

She kissed him on the cheek and stepped back, giving him a lost puppy look. "Sometimes things happen. It's not like I had a choice in any of it."

"Can you at least tell me the size of the knife?"

She held her hands out, spacing them apart to match the length of Jack's Ka-Bar knife. "About so, and it had a serrated edge near the handle."

"Like a hunting knife?"

"More like an Army knife. You know, the really scary kind."

"And it just disappeared all on its own?"

"Like I said, it all happened so fast. No telling what happened to it."

"You know that's weak, right? I mean really weak. The kind of weak that gets people tossed into jail. And other people fired."

"Nice try, brother. But you and I both know that you won't let any of that happen."

"Of course not, but I still need an explanation for everything."

Elsa shrugged, unsure of what to say.

"Army, huh?" Lyle asked before he walked to the trunk of his sedan and popped it open. His arm went inside and when it came back out, he held up a knife that was about the same size as Jack's. It even had a serrated edge. "Something like this?"

"Yeah, that's almost it exactly."

"Almost?"

"No, that's it. I'm sure. Except the handle. It was a different color," she answered, thinking about the initials J.T. on the side of Jack's knife.

"When you said Army, it made me think of Burt. He left this in the back of my truck after we gutted that elk last month. Just haven't had a chance to get it back to him."

"Yeah, that was some good meat. Especially the way you marinated it first."

Lyle held for a moment, his eyes looking as though he was in the middle of some decision. A moment later, he turned his neck and peered off into the distance, looking in the same direction as Jack had walked, almost as if he had a sixth sense about what had happened.

She kept calm and silent, not wanting to give him any indication that he might be onto something.

When he brought his eyes back to her, he said, "Hold out your hands for me."

She did as he asked, extending them toward him with her palms up.

He motioned at her. "Now turn them over."

She did. "What?"

"Just checking for blood."

"Ah, well, I wiped it off before you got here."

"Yeah, sure. If you say so, sis. On what?"

"I don't remember exactly. It all—"

"—happened so fast. Yeah, I heard you the first three times you said that. And I suppose you were able to calm your adrenaline instantly as well."

"You know I don't get nervous easily."

"This isn't about nervousness. This is about my sister killing some guy with her bare hands."

"You mean with a knife."

"Yeah, same thing. Plus, you apparently then decided to beat the other guy and break his nose. A guy that's twice your size, like some kind of ninja chick who's been secretly training all these years."

"If only," she said, unable to think of anything else to say.

"Usually the perpetrator can't keep his hands still for hours—sometimes the rest of the day. It's just human nature. Especially the guilt part. Unless, of course, it was premeditated and the suspect is a serial killer."

"Yeah, right. Now who's going off the deep end?" she said, rolling her eyes at him. "I told you it was self-defense. What's there to feel guilty about?"

He stood there blinking for what seemed like a minute, maybe two, in complete silence.

Elsa had to say something; the silence was eating at her gut. "Sorry about all this. I know it's a big ask, but—"

Lyle threw up his hands. "Why didn't you tell me about these guys hassling you?"

"Honestly, I never thought they'd go this far. Plus, you were busy with all your sheriff stuff."

"Exactly. Sheriff stuff. Like helping my little sister deal with the town assholes. I could have stopped all of this before it ever started."

"How? You know what Clive is like. He's old school. Guys like that don't listen to anyone," she replied, realizing she was mostly talking about herself.

"Except the law. That's what I'm here for. What kind of Sheriff would I be if I can't step in and help my sister?"

"That's exactly what you're doing right now. And I love you all the more for it."

He shook his head. "Why should I be surprised? You always know what buttons to push, sis."

"It's called family. It's only a matter of time before we know each other's buttons. And secrets. All of them."

"Ain't that the truth."

"So we're good?"

"I'm not even sure what that means anymore."

She didn't respond.

Lyle continued, "The hard part is going to be explaining this to the Mayor. He's gonna want answers. So is Clive."

"You'll think of something. You always do."

"It's probably best if we just say you came home and found these guys in your road. That's all you know."

"If you think so. Sure. I can play dumb. I'm just a poor, helpless farm girl out here in the country."

310

"It's better than saying that you just got lucky. Seriously, sis. That'll never fly."

"What about Dwayne?"

Lyle scoffed. "Don't worry about him. He'll say whatever I tell him to say."

"More secrets, I take it?"

"His worse than yours. Seems like all I do anymore is damage control for my friends."

"And family," she replied.

"But all those IOUs do come in handy now and then."

She agreed. "What about Tony? Eventually they're going to unscramble his brains. His version will be different than mine."

"That habitual liar? I doubt anyone will believe him. That's assuming he says Jack."

"Jack? What do you mean?"

"I mean he's old school, like you said. They'll never involve the law. It's a pride thing."

"So they're going to handle it themselves."

"I'm afraid so."

"Shit, he was right," Elsa mumbled, unable to stop the words from leaving her lips.

"I'm sorry, what?"

"Nothing. Just talking to myself."

"Who's he? Who are you talking about?"

"Never you mind, now," she said, thinking of Tony in the back seat of the deputy's car. "Maybe we should have called an ambulance?"

"For Tony?"

"He needs to see a doctor."

"Dwayne will handle it. Trust me."

She shrugged. "You're the Sheriff."

"Besides, the last thing we needed was more witnesses."

"I get that. But still, it might have gone over better with Clive if we—"

"Look, sis. Nothing is gonna polish this pig. It is what it is. Now we deal with the aftermath," Lyle said. "Which is why I'm gonna station a couple of deputies here."

"For how long?"

"Till this blows over."

"And when will that be?"

"Who knows? But I doubt it will take long."

"Great, just what I need."

"You should have thought about all of that before you decided to take matters into your own hands."

"I told you before, it was self-defense. I didn't plan any of this."

"Just so you know, everyone says that."

"But I'm your sister. You know me."

Lyle nodded once, took off his hat, then climbed into the driver's seat. "If anything else happens, like the IRS shows up, or your truck starts making a weird noise, or a spaceship lands in your back yard with three-headed aliens, call me. Please. Let me take care of it before I *have* to take care of it."

"I will. Promise. Just a run of bad luck, that's all."

He eased back into the seat and picked up the microphone hanging on a hook along the dash, then brought it to his lips.

She watched him press transmit and open his mouth to speak, but then he released the button and sat frozen in the seat.

"What's wrong, Lyle?"

"I hope you know there's no going back once I make this call."

CHAPTER 24

"Well, this doesn't look too promising," Ben said, hoisting the mountain bike to Marcus on the dock. He climbed out of the boat and planted his shoes on the wooden planks, feeling a sway beneath his feet. "Place looks like a ghost town."

"Where is everyone?" Tess asked, working the leash to keep Wilma away from the boatman.

"Where's the ATM from here?" Marcus asked.

Ben pointed, aiming his finger just beyond a shop he knew to contain Amish Furniture. "I think it's down that street over there, but it's been a while, so hopefully it's still there."

"It better be. I want my three grand."

When Marcus turned his head to peer in the direction of the street, Ben flashed an intense look at Tess, hoping she'd know what the gesture meant.

She nodded back, angling her head a few degrees and sending her eyes in the opposite direction from where Marcus was focused.

Ben gave her a nod, then held out a hand, palm down with his fingers spread, flaring his eyebrows in the process.

She seemed to understand, wrapping the leash a few more times around her palm.

They walked as a group for about two hundred yards, then took the next left and headed along a sidewalk that bordered the next street.

Again, there were no people. Only a few cars sitting alone, two of which had their hoods up. One was left with its passenger door open and a smashed bag of potato chips sitting on the asphalt.

"This is starting to look familiar," Ben said to Marcus, but looking at Tess.

She nodded but didn't respond.

"So where is it?" Marcus asked.

"Another couple of blocks, I think. Like I said, been a while."

"Is that smoke?" Tess asked, pointing ahead and to the right.

Ben brought his eyes to bear, hearing some glass breaking. "Sounds like trouble up there."

"Ah, nice try," Marcus said, "but we're not turning around."

He put a hand into the back of his waistband and when he pulled it out, his fingers wrapped around a handgun. It wasn't very big. Probably a .380 caliber, Ben figured. However, if it were loaded with Critical Defense rounds, then the hollow points would still do significant damage to whatever target Marcus chose.

"Hey, what's with the gun?" Tess asked.

"You know, just in case. Can't be too careful these days," Marcus said, raising the pistol into a firing position and aiming it at the noise ahead.

Ben wasn't sure if that 'just in case' comment was meant for him and Tess, or the people ahead. "Maybe you should take the lead, Marcus."

The man increased his pace, moving three steps in front of Tess and Wilma, with the gun still raised.

Ben moved alongside Tess, putting a soft hand on her forearm.

Tess slowed her pace as Marcus continued with his, his eyes apparently locked downrange.

316

When an adjacent street came into view, Ben saw the source of the glass breakage and smoke—a pawn shop. It was on fire with a crowd of about fifteen people milling about in front of it. "Well, that explains it."

"Fucking assholes. Always taking to the streets and wrecking their own neighborhoods. I don't understand any of it," Marcus said.

"Yeah, me either," Ben replied, moving his hand in front of Tess.

She stopped. So did Wilma.

Ben pointed at an open door across the street while Marcus was looking elsewhere. The sign on the window said *Keystone Hot Tubs*. Ben pointed at her in silence and then at the open door.

She nodded and changed direction, heading for the open door with Wilma.

Ben increased his speed to stay close to Marcus and keep him distracted. "What's the plan?"

"Well, I either start shooting these pricks or we work our way behind them," Marcus replied, turning his head to look at Ben.

Ben moved a step to the side, making sure he kept his body between Marcus and the area directly behind, where he envisioned Tess and Wilma were walking. "I vote for the latter. The bank's just ahead. Past a One-Hour Clinic, if I remember right."

Marcus returned his eyes to the throng of looters, angling his feet to begin a wide course around the crowd.

Thirty steps later, they had made it about halfway behind the mob without anyone noticing their activity.

That's when Ben decided to fake a sneeze.

Marcus turned his head and gawked at Ben with his eyes wide.

Ben shrugged as some of the looters turned and looked in their direction. Ben shoved Marcus from behind, sending the man forward a step. "Run!"

Marcus took off straight ahead, while Ben turned and ran in the opposite direction.

Ben pointed back at Marcus and yelled to the horde, "He's got cash on him. Lots of it."

Four members of the looters turned their focus to Marcus and chased after him. The rest of the gang stayed glued to their pawn shop activities.

Ben looked back.

Nobody was chasing him.

He kept his speed up until he made it to the door of the hot tub store, where he ducked inside and closed the door behind him.

When he scanned the darkened room, he found Tess standing with a couple wearing bright yellow company polo shirts and jeans. Both were in their late forties, if he had to guess.

Wilma was there, too, standing a foot or two beyond the corner of the main reception counter.

Tess ran over to Ben and hugged him.

Wilma trotted along.

Ben let go of her. "Who are these people?"

"The owners. Charlie and Diane."

Ben sent a head nod at Charlie.

The man gave him a quick wave back.

Ben brought his attention to Tess. "Why was the door open?"

"Their daughter just left to go get help. I guess we barely missed her."

"I take it the phones are out?"

"Yep, they tried to call 911 but couldn't."

"Then it must have been high altitude, like we thought, to cover this much area."

319

The man behind the counter stepped forward. "High altitude what?"

"EMP, I'm thinking. That's why everything is out."

Charlie held for a moment, then nodded. "Which would explain why there are no alarms going off at the pawn shop."

"Yes, and the looters know it."

"Good thing thieves don't want hot tubs," Charlie said to Diane.

She brought her hands together in front of her chest and looked up. "Yes, thank God."

"Or they're just too big to carry," Ben said, unable to stop the words from leaving his mouth. He didn't want to belittle their obvious faith in the almighty, but the words needed to be said, regardless.

"So here and the cabin?" Tess asked.

"Unfortunately."

"Then it's probably happening in Seattle, too."

Ben nodded. "Seems likely. And Bell Hill."

"Wow, that means the whole state."

"Maybe. But like I said before, these things are typically line of sight. So it might just be in this general area."

"Makes sense either way."

"Yeah, but something tells me there are probably other areas, too. We just don't know yet."

"Or they're next?" Charlie said. "Assuming this is no accident."

"Been a lot of *accidents* lately," Tess said, rolling her eyes at Ben.

"Well, based on what I remember from my days back in the service, I suppose someone might be purposely taking out the enemy's communications and ability to supply," Ben said, working it through his mind.

"Enemy, as in us?" Tess asked.

"I'm afraid so. Start in one location and work your way to the next."

"Perhaps this is all a prelude of some kind?" Charlie said, his tone elevating in pitch. "In advance of something else?"

"Could be," Ben said, shrugging. "Either way, you two should still leave. That crowd might work its way here, eventually."

Charlie nodded. "Can we go with you?"

"I don't think that's a g—" Ben started to say.

"Ben, we can't just leave them here," Tess said. "Please. It's the right thing to do."

Ben knew she was right, but he still didn't want to agree. "Okay, they can come with. But only for a couple of blocks. Otherwise, they'll just slow us down."

Charlie and Diane walked out from behind the counter. "Where you two headed?"

"Bell Hill," Tess said.

"My old man's place."

Tess nodded. "Hopefully, he's there, waiting for us."

CHAPTER 25

Elsa turned the John Deere backhoe tractor and headed for the barn, thinking of Jack and all that had happened the day before.

Her mind couldn't seem to decide what to focus on, alternating between visions of Jack and his killer smile and the knife sticking out of Sam's neck. Talk about life running hot and cold—both types of flashes intense and neither of them going away anytime soon.

Lyle hadn't gotten back to her since he made the call. Not that silence from him was all that unusual. Sometimes they'd go weeks without a text or phone call, but she thought with all that had transpired in front of her property, he'd at least reach out. If nothing else, check in with his deputy out front.

Last time she checked, Dwayne was still parked beyond the main gate, sitting in his patrol car with his head against the headrest and his cap low over his eyes, enjoying the shade provided by the oldest tree on her property.

She'd gotten to know the guy a little bit the week before when she called in a nuisance report about the crop circle in the middle of her eastern-most corn field.

The mashed down area scared her at first, not realizing what it was when she happened upon it. Then it dawned on her what she was looking at.

Stupid kids, though it was impressive how perfectly they'd made the circle and bent over the stalks. Not a single one of them broken.

She figured Lyle was probably busy putting out another fire somewhere. Another needy soul. Another friend's mess to fix. Or maybe he was sitting with the Mayor and explaining her predicament. She didn't know and it really didn't matter. Lyle would do what Lyle needed to do. As would she.

Elsa parked the tractor to the left of the barn, not far from the base of the water tower, then lowered the front bucket to release the hydraulic pressure on the lines, killed the engine with the toggle switch next to her knee, and took off her padded earmuffs.

She hung the headset over the bottom of the steering wheel then rubbed her earlobes, hoping the blood would return to them soon.

Elsa might have chosen to work the fields each day, but unlike some of her elderly neighbors, she wasn't going to damage her hearing in the process. Especially with diesel engines that were beyond loud. More so when you're sitting only a few feet behind a puttering ninety-horsepower, turbo-charged beast.

A girl had to make choices, and saving her hearing was one of them.

So was stopping and giving Jack a ride yesterday. A man with as many tattoos as secrets, she figured.

She may not have known him well or long, but one thing was certain—he was a man of action. And had a serious thing for bandages. Whatever had happened to his neck must have hurt, but she never asked him about it. It really wasn't her place.

Elsa hopped off the open-cab backhoe and stretched her back, feeling the aftereffects of the nonstop rocking motion from the oversized rear tires.

Every roll. Every rut. Every bump. All of it injected into her spine thanks to the thirty-two pounds of pressure she kept in them at all times.

There may have been other farmers in the county who could sit and ride all day without pain, but she wasn't one of them. But it was her decision to take on this farm, so she needed to suck it up.

"Time to feed the hogs," she mumbled, appreciating that statement more than ever before.

Who knew a skinny girl could handle the rigors of taking care of animals and riding a tractor for hours?

She didn't, but then again, challenges were something she liked to think she could take head-on. So was learning new things, like the fact that some light-colored pigs actually got sunburned. Talk about a surprise.

The pigpen holding her hogs was a hundred yards away and nestled up against the back side of her equipment barn. In retrospect, it probably wasn't the best location to build the enclosure, not with the biblical smell wafting its way onto every piece of machinery she owned.

It was her hope that she'd eventually get used to the stench. At least that's what she kept telling herself. So far, it hadn't happened.

She changed her thoughts to Jack and his amazing shoulders as she made the first corner of her barn, heading north toward the rear to make sure her pigs had food and water for the day.

When she was about halfway there, a figure stepped out from beyond the far end of the wall.

It was a man with a white bandage across his nose and one hand behind his back.

She recognized the muscular man and his crooked smile. It was Tony, his eyes swollen and black and blue.

"Shit," she muttered, stopping her feet.

"Miss me, bitch?"

Elsa held up her hands. "Look, I don't want any trouble."

Tony brought his hand out from behind his back, revealing a machete. "You mean like this?"

"Wait. Wait. Wait. Let's talk about this," she said, backing up and wishing her mind would focus on something other than that blade gleaming in the sunlight.

So far, Tony didn't look to be in a hurry to hack her to pieces. It was more like he was content to creep forward, looking the part of slayer, not actually being one.

Then again, maybe she was just trying to convince herself that was true.

One look at the man and certain facts became clear—she was younger and lighter, which gave her an idea.

Maybe she could outrun him?

At least long enough to make it to Dwayne out front?

It wouldn't be the first time she'd made a run for it. But it might be her last if she couldn't muster enough speed or courage to make it happen.

Right then was when she heard it.

A crunch of dirt behind her.

Then someone clearing their throat.

She stopped her feet and turned to see another man, this one freakishly tall, with an all-white beard that hung down to his chest. Plus, he had more wrinkles on his face than a seven-foot-tall unmade bed.

Elsa recognized him.

It was Tony's Uncle Clive, standing there with bowed legs, a curved back, and three teeth missing along the front. "It be time for a little payback."

"You stay away from me," Elsa snapped, her eyes now locked with his.

Clive brought his hand up, with his fingers wrapped in a wad of hair that was attached to a severed head. It was still dripping blood. "Thought you be safe, did you?"

"Oh my God, is that Dwayne?"

"He should've looked behind him once in a while," Clive said, his hillbilly voice as old and gravelly as the skin across his cheeks. He snorted a quick laugh. "Just be sitting there like he was all dat."

She held up her hands and let the tears fly. "Please. Don't do this. Please. I'll do whatever you want."

"It be too late for dat, missy. You had ya chance. More dan once, I might add. Then you go about killing my kin. Folks in these parts don't take too kindly to dat."

Elsa turned to the right and screamed at her legs to get moving. They listened and began a full-on sprint toward the closest cornfield.

She knew the full-sized stalks would help conceal her, but they'd also break upon impact, giving these men a trail to follow.

It wasn't a great plan, but it was her only plan.

CHAPTER 26

Run. Run. Run, Elsa told herself, pumping her arms and legs faster than she ever thought possible. She brought her hands up, trying to block an assembly line of cornstalks smashing into her face.

She could feel the slits and tears on her skin around her wrists and forearms, but she didn't dare stop. Not to check. Not to breathe. Not to look back, either.

When the cornfield gave way to a clearing that used to be smothered with bent stalks, she knew where she was—in the middle of the crop circle that the local kids had made the week before.

The pile of stalks she'd gathered that morning was still there, waiting to be fed to the hogs after pitchforking them into the dumpster she'd brought in with the backhoe only an hour before. For some

331

reason, her mind decided to wonder about the odds of her jaunt bringing her here, to this exact location.

The sound of footsteps crunching cornstalks took her from her thoughts, but the noise was not just coming at her from the rear. It was also ahead of her and to the right, sounding as though there was a herd of men approaching.

"Shit." They seemed to be closing in from every direction.

Elsa ran to the pile of stalks and grabbed the handle of the pitchfork that was sticking straight up. She pulled it free in a yank, then turned it around in her hands, holding it out in front of her like a spear. Her hands shook as she listened to the sounds trampling the field ahead of her, behind her, and to the right.

There was no way she could fight them all but maybe, just maybe, if she impaled one of these guys in the face, the others might think twice.

A heartbeat later, one of the men appeared from the front. It was Clive, the freak who stood as tall as a windmill.

He must have been able to see the stalks swaying as she ran, allowing him swing around and come at her from the north. It also meant the old guy was fast. Faster than her.

She doubled her grip on the implement, making sure the spikes were aimed at Clive. "Don't come any closer or I'll kill you."

"You think that gonna stop me? Think again," Clive said, lifting his shirt and showing her a litany of scars across his belly and chest. He looked like a pincushion for the damned.

Clive dropped his shirt, then charged at her, letting out some kind of hillbilly grunt she hadn't heard before.

Just then a flash of movement broke through from the cornstalks on the right and flew at Clive, raising a fist in the process. It was a man. A big man. Tattooed. Bandages on his neck.

"Jack?" she mumbled as Bunker landed an overhead punch on the side of Clive's head, sending the guy flying in a rolling tumble of arms and legs.

Clive came to rest face down, with one of his arms trapped under his body. He lifted his head and shook it, then pried his arm free as Jack ran at him.

When Clive began to press to his feet, Jack landed a kick to his stomach, making Clive gasp and flip over onto his back.

Jack drew his knife from his hip and held it high as he pounced on Clive like what Elsa could only describe as a centerfielder diving for a ball in the gap.

Just as Jack rammed the tip of his knife into Clive's throat, Elsa heard another noise. This time from the rear.

She spun to see Tony break free from the stalks in a stumbling, broken trot, still holding the machete.

The muscle-bound guy then bent over at the waist, his chest pumping for air like there wasn't any left. A few gulps later, he straightened up and raised the weapon, then said in a breathy voice, "You bastards. I gonna kill you."

"Jack, a little help here," Elsa called out as Tony came at her.

She raised the pitchfork, planning to stick one of the three tines into Tony's neck, just like Jack had done to Clive.

When Tony arrived, Elsa shoved the pitchfork at him, but he brought his free arm up only a split second before she made contact.

The leftmost spike stuck into his forearm as he swung it to the side, sending Elsa along with it.

She couldn't stop her momentum, letting go of the farm implement and hitting the ground in an awkward flop.

Elsa turned onto her back and looked up to see Tony yank the fork out of his arm and toss it away as if it had never happened. Then he moved above her with the machete raised in a striking position.

His lips pinched and his face turned red as he brought the blade down in a blur.

She spun her shoulders and rolled to the left, hearing the steel whiz past her ear and hit the dirt.

A moment later, she felt pressure on her shoulder from above. When her eyes came around, she watched Tony's hand spin her onto her back.

She tried to punch his arm away, but her blows only bounced off the goliath's skin.

Tony dropped down, pressing his kneecap into the middle of her chest. "Not this time, bitch."

When he raised the machete for another strike, she held her hands up and closed her eyes, knowing he wouldn't miss this time—not from close range and not while pinning her to the ground.

Time seemed to slow down a hundred-fold as she waited for the pain to come.

Eventually, she did feel something but it wasn't pain. It was a rocking motion, from left to right, as a sudden lurching *oomph* rang in her ears.

She opened her eyes to see Jack wrestling with Tony in a battle for the machete.

Elsa got to her feet and backed up, watching the two men spin like logs on a river, their biceps bulging as if they were balloons ready to burst.

"You killed my cousin, asshole," Tony said in a grunting voice after they stopped rolling with Tony on top.

"Watch out," Elsa said, seeing Tony tilt the tip of the blade toward Jack, even though all four of their hands were wrapped around each other in what she could only describe as a death grip.

Jack didn't respond to her warning, instead bringing a leg up and around the front of Tony, latching onto his torso. A second later, Tony toppled backwards under the pressure of Jack's thigh.

They kept their hands on the machete as Tony's spine hit the ground. Their collective momentum must have been strong since it seemed to rock Jack up on top of Tony, with the machete out to the side.

"Now who's the asshole, asshole?" Jack asked.

Tony's face turned an even darker shade of red before he said, "I'm gonna bleed you, boy."

That's when the machete began to move again, this time from the side to the middle as Tony appeared to be getting the upper hand.

When Tony turned the blade toward Jack again and inched it closer, Elsa ran to the pitchfork that had been tossed away. She snatched it up and ran back to the men, turning the tines down and raising the handle.

When she saw the machete start to penetrate Jack's shirt, she yelled, "Lean back, Jack."

She felt a sudden wave of energy fill her body as she brought the pitchfork down in one massive thrust, aiming it at Tony's face.

When the middle spike made contact, it didn't land where she planned. Instead, it impaled Tony's throat, dead center into the man's Adam's apple.

Tony's hands let go of the machete and went to his neck, as he gagged in obvious pain for what she assumed was air.

Jack jumped off the man, spun the machete around, then brought it down in a chop, landing it just below the point where the pitchfork had met skin.

Tony's throat split open, sending blood out in spurts.

Jack brought the machete up for a second strike and held it, looking at Elsa.

"Do it," she said. "Do it, now."

Jack gave her an affirmative look with his eyes, then brought the blade down with even more speed than before.

This time the strike liberated Tony's head from his body, leaving only a corpse shooting blood.

Elsa backed away.

So did Jack, the two of them standing shoulder to shoulder and watching the spectacle run red with blood. It took about twenty seconds for the spurting to stop, leaving a good-sized pool of red in the dirt.

"Geez, what a mess," Elsa said, looking down at the results.

"That's all you have to say?"

"What do you mean?"

"Most people react a little differently."

"You mean, like freak out."

"For one."

"I'm a farmer, remember. Seen my share of animals decapitated. And trust me, this guy was an animal. At least he isn't running around without his head attached."

"Still, that's a pretty gruesome thing to witness."

"I'll be all right. Besides, we really didn't have a choice, now did we?"

"About taking them out? No. How we did it? Some might argue yes."

"I guess I better call my brother. He's manning the phones today at the Sheriff's office."

"No brother. No Sheriff. Not this time."

"We have to, Jack. It's the right thing."

"This time, we do it my way. No evidence. No witnesses. No cover-ups."

She shook her head, but remained silent.

"I'm deadly serious here. We have to deal with this once and for all. Are you with me?"

Again, she held her tongue, unsure what to say.

"Elsa, I need you to trust me right now. Do you?"

"Yes, of course. Completely."

"Then we deal with the bodies, now."

"Okay, how do we do that exactly?"

"You have a chainsaw, right?"

"Yeah, but the chain is broken."

"Anything else?"

"Well, there's an old portable sawmill out back that used to be used for cutting up oak trees by the previous owner. If we can get it working—"

"The bandsaw will work."

Elsa nodded. "What do we do with all the parts?"

"Good question."

She put her hands on her hips and changed to a matter-of-fact tone of voice. "Well, I've got two hundred acres and a backhoe we could use. All we have to do is pick a spot."

Bunker paused for a good ten seconds. "No, that'll still leave evidence for someone to find."

She nodded, running the rest of that discovery through her mind. "Not to mention a fresh hole."

"What about your pigs? They eat anything, right?"

"Just about."

"Bone, too?"

"As far as I know," Elsa said, understanding where he was going with his thinking. "Plus their slop will cover up any smell or blood."

"That's what I was thinking. We'll have to go find their vehicle and dispose of it somewhere."

"Could drive it into Salt Lake and leave it at the airport."

"That might work. But we'll need to go to their house and pack up some of their stuff. Do you know where they live?"

She pointed. "On the other side of the county."

"All right, we go there tonight. Get in. Get out. Get it done."

"Then you'll be on your way, right? For sure this time?"

Bunker pulled out a slip of paper from his pocket and held it up. "I have a train to catch, remember?"

"Then I have your word? You'll actually leave this time and never come back?"

EPILOGUE

Jack Bunker leaned his head back against the padded headrest of the Amtrak train as it chugged its way higher through the countryside of the majestic Rocky Mountains.

He kept his eyes turned to the right and focused on the colorful tapestry rolling past the passenger window, knowing all the while that a pair of piercing blue eyes was locked onto his face by the fidgeting young boy sitting across from him.

The stare-down began an hour ago, when an attractive soccer mom and her redheaded son decided to share the adjoining seat in the sightseeing car.

Bunker didn't blame the kid. Curiosity was part of a young person's nature, especially when confronted with a tall stranger wearing playing-card-sized bandages across both sides of his neck.

Fortunately, Bunker's long-sleeve t-shirt covered up his chest, back, and arms, keeping his self-indulgent political statements hidden from the rest of the planet.

If Bunker had to guess, he'd estimate the inquisitive boy was around ten years old. The freckles across his cheeks and nose may have been thin, but his weight was a tad thick.

"Excuse me, mister. What does that mean?" the kid asked, pointing at the three tattooed letters on Bunker's knuckles. "What's B-T-F?"

The kid's mother—a pretty, voluptuous blonde woman in her late 20s—didn't interject or stop the intrusion, so Bunker decided to answer the lad.

"It means Born To Fight. Something my dad used to say to me when I was about your age."

"Did it hurt when your dad put those letters on your hand?"

"No, son. I had those letters tattooed on when I joined the Marines. I did it to honor my father's memory after he passed away."

"I think I want some letters, too," the boy said, swinging his eyes up to his mother, who was seated next to him.

She didn't answer her son, seemingly more interested in the iPad sitting on her lap.

Ever since she'd sat down, her cell phone never seemed to stop chiming from yet another text message. Working her technology was keeping her too busy to notice his obvious cover-up with the bandages, or her son's questions.

Yet she wasn't the only one who was distracted.

Most of the other rail riders had their eyes focused on the countryside streaming past the windows at a steep incline, or had their heads buried in their portable tech, too.

Bunker wondered what the rest of the passengers would think if they knew who they were traveling with.

It had been two months of off-the-radar wandering since he'd left behind his past and went in search of a new life.

So far, he hadn't found what he was looking for, but at least his jet-black hair had made a full comeback, resuming its sweeping fullness.

He'd almost forgotten what it was like to have something to comb after running bald for what seemed like forever. He planned to keep it simple by slicking it straight back, at least for now.

Next up, he needed to find a new, stress-free life that would match his simple hairstyle. He wasn't sure where he was going when he got on this train, but he figured he'd know it once he arrived.

When you start a fresh journey into the unknown, it helps to allow random luck to select your path.

If not, then you run the risk of letting old habits and burnt-in thought patterns influence the decision-making process.

When that happens, it increases the chances of falling right back into the same swirl of discontent from which you are trying to escape.

At least, that's what he hoped for himself by letting fate guide him to this place and time.

His decision to find a new life started with an off-the-books name change and the selling of his most prized asset for cash, clothes, and a few supplies, most of which were stuffed into an army surplus duffel bag stowed in the overhead bin.

He'd gone minimalist by shedding most of what made him, him. At least the old him. Hopefully, this reboot would change everything.

Bunker had been walking the back roads mostly, though he'd caught a few rides from generous strangers who'd stopped to see if he needed any help.

He didn't have his thumb out hitchhiking, nor was he asking for help. They just stopped on their own to make sure he was okay, and that surprised him. And gave him hope for the cesspool known as society.

Two months of mostly anonymous travels had taught him a few things already.

One of which was that when you immerse yourself in the reality of rural, off-the-radar living, you can actually feel the difference in the atmosphere around you.

Not just with the crystal clean air entering your lungs, but in the way the air cradles your soul, allowing you to absorb a more casual, free lifestyle through the pores in your skin.

"Excuse me, sir," the slender yet curvy woman with the plunging neckline said, finally speaking up after leaning forward and touching his forearm from across the gap between the seats.

Bunker kept his eyes in check, even though her abundance of cleavage was screaming at him to look down.

"Yes," he said, giving her a thin smile and a quick nod. He didn't want to have a conversation with anyone at the moment, but if he was going to become a new and improved version of himself, then it was time to engage the rest of civilization. Like any normal person would.

"Do you happen to know when we're supposed to pull into the Denver station?" she asked.

"I'm guessing about two hours, give or take. Gonna take a while to climb some of these hills. They're pretty steep. You can really hear the engine chugging now."

"Two hours? I don't think my bladder is going to hold out that long."

He wondered why she didn't know the schedule already. Unless she relocated from another seat on the train, he assumed she'd just gotten on the train at the previous stop.

Maybe she was in a hurry when she purchased the ticket and didn't have a chance to memorize the stops. "You do realize there's a head at the rear of the car, right? No reason to hold it."

"Yeah, I know. But have you seen it? It's a unisex bathroom and it's disgusting. No offense, but you men can't seem to ever hit what you aim at. Especially my ex-husband. He was the worst. I swear he did it on purpose, just to push my buttons."

Bunker nodded. She was right. Most of the men on the planet were pigs, and on so many levels. The least of which was spraying the seat when taking a leak.

If she only knew the kind of men Bunker used to run with, then she'd truly understand what constituted an asshole and a disgusting bathroom. The shitter at his last job was biblical. Talk about ripe.

When a series of memory flashes from his past decided to dance front and center in his mind, he couldn't help but offer up a smirk.

The woman's eyes lit up with energy after she leaned her head back. "Just once, I'd like to walk into a shared bathroom and not have to bring a stack of wipes and can of Lysol with me. I mean seriously, is that too much to ask?"

He wanted to verbally agree with her, but before he could think of something clever to say, the overhead lights in the car blinked out and the train began to slow. The only remaining light in the train car was the sunlight beaming in through the windows.

"That's weird," she said, flashing a look of confusion. The woman fiddled with the iPad screen, then checked her cell phone. "How could both of them be dead?"

"Mine too, Mommy," the boy added, holding up his videogame unit in front of her eyes.

When the kid turned it around, Jack realized it wasn't a game after all. It was an educational system with a blank screen in the center and a series of raised, multiple choice buttons across the bottom. The stamped metal nameplate at the top said *Frankie's Science Lab*.

Bunker turned his eyes from the kid's device and ran a quick visual survey of the passengers with electronics in his vicinity. Each of them looked to be either confused or concerned.

He heard a smattering of "what the hell?", "stupid battery", and "this cell phone never works right" comments, plus a few other, more colorful phrases that the young boy across from him should not have heard.

The locomotive continued to slow until it came to a complete stop, thanks to the steep incline and the pull of gravity.

"You've got to be kidding me," a portly man with a bad comb-over job said from Bunker's left, throwing up his hands in disgust. His wrinkled pinstripe suit and loose-fitting tie screamed businessman heading home to Denver. "My wife is going to be pissed. She hates it when I make her wait at the terminal."

"I wonder if they stopped for something on the tracks, sis," an elderly woman said. She was sitting with a woman who looked like her twin. Both of them were in their 80s and sporting scarves, sweaters, saggy skin, and liver-spotted cheeks.

The woman's sister spun her head and said, "I don't think so, Dolores. Why would the power be out?"

"Don't you remember, Dottie? That's what happened last year on our Alaskan cruise when the engines quit."

"Yes, I remember. Their generators went down when the engine stopped."

Bunker stood up in a flash and stepped into the center aisle. Something was nagging at him to head to the engine room and see what was happening.

"Where are you going?" the blonde woman asked, still seated.

He wasn't sure why she was asking since it wasn't any of her business, but he decided not to be rude. "I gotta go check on something."

"Can I go with him, Mommy?"

"No, Jeffrey. Little boys don't go off with men they don't know. Remember what I told you about stranger danger?"

"Yeah, but I wanna go see, Mom."

"No honey, it's best if you stay here with me. Where it's safe."

"Geez, ever since you kicked Dad out, I never get to do anything fun."

Bunker was about to turn for the exit, but something caught his eye outside. High in the sky and banking left was a commercial airliner. He could see the entire spread of its mighty wingspan, soaring like a metal eagle in search of prey.

It was moving slower than expected and dropping in altitude. The turn looked to be controlled, but the speed of its descent was much too fast. The hairs on the back of his neck started to tingle. Something was wrong. He could feel it.

He checked, but didn't see any sign of smoke trailing behind it. Nor was there any indication of a mid-air collision in the sky around it.

While the stark white plane continued its steep turn, he ran a quick trajectory check of its course. A second later he realized it was headed straight for them, on an apparent intercept vector with the train.

"Get down!" he shouted to the passengers in the car. "Get down, now!"

Heads turned and a few people flinched, but nobody took his advice.

Bunker pointed out the window. "There's a plane headed right for us!"

The blonde and the friendly boy he was sitting with whipped their heads around and looked out the window. The woman screamed but never took her eyes from airplane headed right for them.

Bunker grabbed her with one hand and the kid with the other, pulling them both to the deck. He covered their bodies and then looked around at the other passengers.

Many of them were now on the floor as well, covering their heads with their hands.

A few were still in their seats, their minds unable to reconcile what their eyes were reporting.

Some passengers were screaming hysterically, while others looked frozen in time and unable to move.

He waited for the roar of the jetliner's engines to reach his ears, but it never came.

Instead, a massive explosion rang out as the floor beneath them began to shake. It felt like an earthquake and the ground tremors were intensifying.

The thunderous sound of twisting metal dwarfed the passengers' cries and screams, leading him to believe a massive fireball was headed their way next.

Soon they'd all be sprayed with jet fuel, burning alive in a metal coffin built for fifty.

When the windows shattered, he sucked in a breath and held it, figuring he'd just taken his last breath.

Jo Nash, Jay J. Falconer, M.L. Banner

TO BE CONTINUED in the Amazon #1 Bestselling novel *Bunker: Born to Fight*, Book 1 in the *Mission Critical Series*.

Please Leave a Review

Please help spread the word about this book by posting a quick review on Amazon and Goodreads.

Our plan is to make this a three-book spinoff series, so please post a review and let us know what you think about this story.

Your feedback will help us determine if we should continue this series or not. So please, post a review and tell us what you think of this story.

Thank you for your help!

Jo Nash, Jay J. Falconer, M.L. Banner

About the Authors

Jay J. Falconer is an award-winning screenwriter and USA Today Bestselling author whose books have hit #1 on Amazon in Action & Adventure, Military Sci-Fi, Post-Apocalyptic, Dystopian, Terrorism Thrillers, Technothrillers, Military Thrillers, Young Adult, and Men's Adventure fiction. He lives in the high mountains of northern Arizona where the brisk, clean air and stunning views inspire his day.

You can find more information about this author and his books at www.JayFalconer.com.

Awards and Accolades:
2020 USA Today Bestselling Book
2018 Winner: Best Sci-Fi Screenplay, Los Angeles Film Awards
2018 Winner: Best Feature Screenplay, New York Film Awards
2018 Winner: Best Screenplay, Skyline Indie Film Festival
2018 Winner: Best Feature Screenplay, Top Indie Film Awards

2018 Winner: Best Feature Screenplay, Festigious International Film Festival - Los Angeles

2018 Winner: Best Sci-Fi Screenplay, Filmmatic Screenplay Awards

2018 Finalist: Best Screenplay, Action on Film Awards in Las Vegas

2018 Third Place: First Time Screenwriters Competition, Barcelona International Film Festival

2019 Bronze Medal: Best Feature Script, Global Independent Film Awards

2017 Gold Medalist: Best YA Action Book, Readers' Favorite International Book Awards

2016 Gold Medalist: Best Dystopia Book, Readers' Favorite International Book Awards

Amazon Kindle Scout Winning Author

Jo Nash

Jo was born and raised in Connecticut and now resides in northern Arizona with her husband, son, pure-white Akita and super grumpy tabby cat.

Jo is a veteran of fiction writing, having spent the last eleven years penning her unique brand of science fiction and fantasy.

After trying to navigate the world of traditional publishing, she began looking for a better opportunity to get her stories into the hands of more readers. That's when she decided to join forces with Jay J. Falconer and write in his Bunker Universe to re-launch her career.

Please Leave a Review

Please help spread the word about this book by posting a quick review on Amazon and Goodreads.

Our plan is to make this a three-book spinoff series, so please post a review and let us know what you think about this story.

Your feedback will help us determine if we should continue this series or not. So please, post a review and tell us what you think of this story.

Thank you for your help!

Made in United States
Orlando, FL
06 October 2024

52419424R00198